NORSE
MYTHOLOGY

NEIL
GAIMAN

BLOOMSBURY
LONDON · OXFORD · NEW YORK · NEW DELHI · SYDNEY

Bloomsbury Publishing, London, Oxford, New York, New Delhi and Sydney

First published in Great Britain in February 2017 by Bloomsbury Publishing Plc
50 Bedford Square, London WC1B 3DP

First published in the USA in February 2017 by W. W. Norton & Company, Inc.,
500 Fifth Avenue, New York, NY 10110

This paperback edition published in March 2018

www.bloomsbury.com

BLOOMSBURY is a registered trademark of Bloomsbury Publishing Plc

Text copyright © Neil Gaiman 2017

A CIP catalogue record for this book is available from the British Library

ISBN 978 1 4088 9195 7

Printed and bound in Great Britain by CPI Group (UK) Ltd, Croydon CR0 4YY

1 3 5 7 9 10 8 6 4 2

To be kept up to date about our authors and books, please visit
www.bloomsbury.com/newsletters and sign up for our newsletters,
including news about Neil Gaiman.

The author's affection for the characters shines out from every page, and the narrative, always crisp and direct, combines an adult's insight with a childlike sense of wonder at the magic of it all; the heroes, the monsters, the giants, the runes. Best of all, the stories remain as fresh and appealing as they were when I first discovered them.

Joanne Harris, *Spectator*

It's virtually impossible to read more than ten words by Neil Gaiman and not wish he would tell you the rest of the story. He is a thesaurus of myth, both original and traditional . . . The halls of Valhalla have been crying out for Neil Gaiman to tell their stories to a new audience. Hopefully, this collection will be just the beginning.

Natalie Haynes, *Observer*

A brisk, bloody retelling of the Norse myths with enough serpents, swords, murderous winters and feasting dragons to dispel all nonsense about the north being a place of cosy, hygge pleasures.

The Times

A gripping, suspenseful and quite wonderful reworking of these famous tales. Once you fall into the rhythm of its glinting prose, you will happily read on and on, in thrall to Gaiman's skilful storytelling.

Washington Post

In reinterpreting the tales so faithfully and with such abundant joy, Gaiman assumes the role of fireside bard, inviting us to sit close on a chilly winter's night and chuckle and wonder along with him.

Financial Times

Superb. Just the thing for the literate fantasy lover and the student of comparative religion and mythology alike.

Kirkus

FOR EVERETT,

OLD STORIES

FOR A NEW BOY.

CONTENTS

CONTENTS

AN
INTRODUCTION

I t's as hard to have a favourite sequence of myths as it is to have a favourite style of cooking (some nights you might want Thai food, some nights sushi, other nights you crave the plain home cooking you grew up on). But if I had to declare a favourite, it would probably be for the Norse myths.

My first encounter with Asgard and its inhabitants was as a small boy, no more than seven, reading the adventures of the Mighty Thor as depicted by American comics artist Jack Kirby, in stories plotted by Kirby and Stan Lee and dialogued by Stan Lee's brother, Larry Lieber. Kirby's Thor was powerful and good-looking, his Asgard a towering science fictional city of imposing buildings and dangerous edifices, his Odin wise and noble, his Loki a sardonic horn-helmeted creature of pure mischief. I loved Kirby's blond hammer-wielding Thor, and I wanted to learn more about him.

I borrowed a copy of *Myths of the Norsemen* by Roger Lancelyn Green and read and reread it with delight and puzzlement: Asgard, in this telling, was no longer a Kirbyesque Future City but was a Viking hall and collection of buildings out on the frozen wastes; Odin the all-father was no longer gentle, wise and irascible, but instead he was brilliant, unknowable and dangerous; Thor was just as strong as the Mighty Thor in the comics, his hammer as powerful, but he was . . . well, honestly, not the brightest of the gods; and Loki was not evil, although he was certainly not a force for good. Loki was . . . complicated.

In addition, I learned, the Norse gods came with their own doomsday: Ragnarok, the twilight of the gods, the end of it all. The gods were going to battle the frost giants, and they were all going to die.

Had Ragnarok happened yet? Was it still to happen? I did not know then. I am not certain now.

It was the fact that the world and the story ends, and the way that it ends and is reborn, that made the gods and the frost giants and the rest of them tragic heroes, tragic villains. Ragnarok made the Norse world linger for me, seem strangely present and current, while other, better-documented systems of belief felt as if they were part of the past, old things.

The Norse myths are the myths of a chilly place, with long, long winter nights and endless summer days, myths of a people who did not entirely trust or even like their gods, although they respected and feared them. As best we can tell, the gods of Asgard came from

Germany, spread into Scandinavia, and then out into the parts of the world dominated by the Vikings—into Orkney and Scotland, Ireland and the north of England —where the invaders left places named for Thor or Odin. In English, the gods have left their names in our days of the week. You can find Tyr the one-handed (Odin's son), Odin, Thor and Frigg, the queen of the gods, in, respectively, Tuesday, Wednesday, Thursday and Friday.

We can see the traces of older myths and older religions in the war and the stories of the truce between the gods of the Vanir and the Aesir. The Vanir appear to have been nature gods, brothers and sisters, less warlike, but perhaps no less dangerous than the Aesir.

It's very likely, or at least a workable hypothesis, that there were tribes of people who worshipped the Vanir and other tribes who worshipped the Aesir, and that the Aesir-worshippers invaded the lands of the Vanir-worshippers, and that they made compromises and accommodations. Gods of the Vanir, like the sister and brother Freya and Frey, live in Asgard with the Aesir. History and religion and myth combine, and we wonder and we imagine and we guess, like detectives reconstructing the details of a long-forgotten crime.

There are so many Norse stories we do not have, so much we do not know. All we have are some myths that have come to us in the form of folktales, in retellings, in poems, in prose. They were written down when

Christianity had already displaced the worship of the Norse gods, and some of the stories we have came to us because people were concerned that if the stories were not preserved, some of the kennings—the usages of poets that referred to events in specific myths—would become meaningless; Freya's tears, for example, was a poetic way of saying "gold". In some of the tales the Norse gods are described as men or as kings or heroes of old, so that the stories could be told in a Christian world. Some stories and poems tell of other stories, or imply other stories, that we simply do not have.

It is, perhaps, as if the only tales of the gods and demi-gods of Greece and Rome that had survived were of the deeds of Theseus and Hercules.

We have lost so much.

There are many Norse goddesses. We know their names and some of their attributes and powers, but the tales, myths and rituals have not come down to us. I wish I could retell the tales of Eir, because she was the doctor of the gods, of Lofn, the comforter, who was a Norse goddess of marriages, or of Sjofn, a goddess of love. Not to mention Vor, goddess of wisdom. I can imagine stories, but I cannot tell their tales. They are lost, or buried, or forgotten.

I've tried my best to retell these myths and stories as accurately as I can, and as interestingly as I can.

Sometimes details in the stories contradict each other. But I hope that they paint a picture of a world and a time.

As I retold these myths, I tried to imagine myself a long time ago, in the lands where these stories were first told, during the long winter nights perhaps, under the glow of the Northern Lights, or sitting outside in the small hours, awake in the unending daylight of midsummer, with an audience of people who wanted to know what else Thor did, and what the rainbow was, and how to live their lives, and where bad poetry comes from.

I was surprised, when I finished the stories and read them as a sequence, to find that they felt like a journey, from the ice and the fire that the universe begins in to the fire and the ice that end the world. Along the way we meet people we would know if we met them, people like Loki and Thor and Odin, and people we want to know so much more about (my favourite of these is Angrboda, Loki's wife among the giants, who gives birth to his monstrous children and who is there in ghost form after Balder is slain).

I did not dare go back to the tellers of Norse myth whose work I had loved, to people like Roger Lancelyn Green and Kevin Crossley-Holland, and reread their stories. I spent my time instead with many different translations of Snorri Sturluson's *Prose Edda*, and with the verses of the *Poetic Edda*, words from nine hundred years ago and before, picking and choosing what tales I wanted to retell and how I wanted to tell them, blending versions of myths from the prose and from the poems. (Thor's visit to Hymir, for example, the way I tell it here, is a hybrid: it begins in the *Poetic Edda*, then adds details of Thor's fishing adventure from Snorri's version.)

My battered copy of *A Dictionary of Northern Mythology*, by Rudolf Simek, translated by Angela Hall, was always invaluable, continually consulted, eye-opening and informative.

Huge thanks go to my old friend Alisa Kwitney for her editorial assistance. She was a fabulous sounding board, always opinionated and forthright, helpful, sensible and smart. She got this book written, mostly by wanting to read the next story, and she helped me make the time to write it in. I'm incredibly grateful to her. Thank you to Stephanie Monteith, whose eagle eyes and Norse knowledge caught several things I might have missed. Thanks also to Amy Cherry at Norton, who suggested that I might want to retell some myths at a lunch on my birthday eight years ago, and who has been, all things considered, the most patient editor in the world.

All mistakes, conclusions jumped to, and odd opinions in this volume are mine and mine alone, and I would not wish anyone else blamed for them. I hope I've retold these stories honestly, but there was still joy and creation in the telling.

That's the joy of myths. The fun comes in telling them yourself—something I warmly encourage you to do, you person reading this. Read the stories in this book, then make them your own, and on some dark and icy winter's evening, or on a summer night when the sun will not set, tell your friends what happened when Thor's hammer was stolen, or how Odin obtained the mead of poetry for the gods . . .

Neil Gaiman

Lisson Grove, London,

May 2016

NORSE
MYTHOLOGY

THE

PLAYERS

Many gods and goddesses are named in Norse mythology. You will meet quite a few of them in these pages. Most of the stories we have, however, concern two gods, Odin and his son Thor, and Odin's blood brother, a giant's son called Loki, who lives with the Aesir in Asgard.

Odin

The highest and the oldest of all the gods is Odin.

Odin knows many secrets. He gave an eye for wisdom. More than that, for knowledge of runes, and for power, he sacrificed himself to himself.

He hung from the world-tree, Yggdrasil, hung there for nine nights. His side was pierced by the point of a spear, which wounded him gravely. The winds clutched at him, buffeted his body as it hung. Nothing did he eat for nine days or nine nights, nothing did he drink. He was alone there, in pain, the light of his life slowly going out.

He was cold, in agony, and on the point of death when

his sacrifice bore dark fruit: in the ecstasy of his agony he looked down, and the runes were revealed to him. He knew them, and understood them and their power. The rope broke then, and he fell, screaming, from the tree.

Now he understood magic. Now the world was his to control.

Odin has many names. He is the all-father, the lord of the slain, the gallows god. He is the god of cargoes and of prisoners. He is called Grimnir and Third. He has different names in every country (for he is worshipped in different forms and in many tongues, but it is always Odin they worship).

He travels from place to place in disguise, to see the world as people see it. When he walks among us, he does so as a tall man, wearing a cloak and hat.

He has two ravens, whom he calls Huginn and Muninn, which mean "thought" and "memory". These birds fly back and forth across the world, seeking news and bringing Odin all the knowledge of things. They perch on his shoulders and whisper into his ears.

When he sits on his high throne at Hlidskjalf, he observes all things, wherever they may be. Nothing can be hidden from him.

He brought war into the world: battles are begun by throwing a spear at the hostile army, dedicating the battle and its deaths to Odin. If you survive in battle, it is with Odin's grace, and if you fall it is because he has betrayed you.

If you fall bravely in war the Valkyries, beautiful battle-maidens who collect the souls of the noble dead, will take you and bring you to the hall known as Valhalla. He will be waiting for you in Valhalla, and there you will drink and fight and feast and battle, with Odin as your leader.

Thor

Thor, Odin's son, is the thunderer. He is straightforward where his father Odin is cunning, good-natured where his father is devious.

Huge he is, and red-bearded, and strong, by far the strongest of all the gods. His might is increased by his belt of strength, Megingjord: when he wears it, his strength is doubled.

Thor's weapon is Mjollnir, a remarkable hammer, forged for him by dwarfs. Its story you will learn. Trolls and frost giants and mountain giants all tremble when they see Mjollnir, for it has killed so many of their brothers and friends. Thor wears iron gloves, which help him to grip the hammer's shaft.

Thor's mother was Jord, the earth goddess. Thor's sons are Modi, the angry, and Magni, the strong. Thor's daughter is Thrud, the powerful.

His wife is Sif, of the golden hair. She had a son, Ullr, before she married Thor, and Thor is Ullr's stepfather. Ullr is a god who hunts with bow and with arrows, and he is the god with skis.

Thor is the defender of Asgard and of Midgard.

There are many stories about Thor and his adventures. You will encounter some of them here.

Loki

Loki is very handsome. He is plausible, convincing, like-able, and far and away the most wily, subtle and shrewd of all the inhabitants of Asgard. It is a pity, then, that there is so much darkness inside him: so much anger, so much envy, so much lust.

Loki is the son of Laufey, who was also known as Nal, or needle, because she was slim and beautiful and sharp. His father was said to be Farbauti, a giant; his name means "he who strikes dangerous blows", and Farbauti was as dangerous as his name.

Loki walks in the sky with shoes that fly, and he can transform his shape so he looks like other people, or change into animal form, but his real weapon is his mind. He is more cunning, subtler, trickier than any god or giant. Not even Odin is as cunning as Loki.

Loki is Odin's blood brother. The other gods do not know when Loki came to Asgard, or how. He is Thor's friend and Thor's betrayer. He is tolerated by the gods, perhaps because his stratagems and plans save them as often as they get them into trouble.

Loki makes the world more interesting but less safe. He is the father of monsters, the author of woes, the sly god.

Loki drinks too much, and he cannot guard his words or his thoughts or his deeds when he drinks. Loki and his children will be there for Ragnarok, the end of everything, and it will not be on the side of the gods of Asgard that they will fight.

BEFORE
THE BEGINNING,
AND AFTER

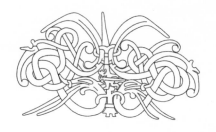

I

Before the beginning there was nothing—no earth, no heavens, no stars, no sky: only the mist world, formless and shapeless, and the fire world, always burning.

To the north was Niflheim, the dark world. Here eleven poisonous rivers cut through the mist, each springing from the same well at the centre of it all, the roaring maelstrom called Hvergelmir. Niflheim was colder than cold, and the murky mist that cloaked everything hung heavily. The skies were hidden by mist and the ground was clouded by the chilly fog.

To the south was Muspell. Muspell was fire. Everything there glowed and burned. Muspell was light where Niflheim was grey, molten lava where the mist world was frozen. The land was aflame with the roaring heat of a blacksmith's fire; there was no solid earth, no sky. Nothing but sparks and spurting heat, molten rocks and burning embers.

In Muspell, at the edge of the flame, where the mist

burns into light, where the land ends, stood Surtr, who existed before the gods. He stands there now. He holds a flaming sword, and the bubbling lava and the freezing mist are as one to him.

It is said that at Ragnarok, which is the end of the world, and only then, Surtr will leave his station. He will go forth from Muspell with his flaming sword and burn the world with fire, and one by one the gods will fall before him.

II

Between Muspell and Niflheim was a void, an empty place of nothingness, without form. The rivers of the mist world flowed into the void, which was called Ginnungagap, the "yawning gap". Over time beyond measure, these poisoned rivers, in the region between fire and mist, slowly solidified into huge glaciers. The ice in the north of the void was covered in frozen fog and pellets of hail, but to the south, where the glaciers reached the land of fire, the embers and the sparks from Muspell met the ice, and warm winds from the flame lands made the air above the ice as gentle and as comfortable as a spring day.

Where the ice and the fire met the ice melted, and in the melting waters life appeared: the likeness of a person bigger than worlds, huger than any giant there will be or has ever been. This was neither male, nor was it female, but was both at the same time.

This creature was the ancestor of all the giants, and it called itself Ymir.

Ymir was not the only living thing to be formed by the melting of the ice: there was also a hornless cow, more enormous than the mind could hold. She licked the salty blocks of ice for food and for drink, and the milk that ran from her four udders flowed like rivers. It was this milk that nourished Ymir.

The giant drank the milk, and grew.

Ymir called the cow Audhumla.

The cow's pink tongue licked people from the blocks of ice: the first day only a man's hair, the second his head, and the third day the shape of a whole man was revealed.

This was Buri, the ancestor of the gods.

Ymir slept, and while it slept, it gave birth: a male and a female giant were born from beneath Ymir's left arm, a six-headed giant born from its legs. From these, Ymir's children, all giants are descended.

Buri took a wife from among these giants, and they had a son, whom they called Bor. Bor married Bestla, daughter of a giant, and together they had three sons: Odin, Vili and Ve.

Odin and Vili and Ve, the three sons of Bor, grew into manhood. They saw as they grew, far off, the flames of Muspell and the darkness of Niflheim, but they knew that each place would be death to them. The brothers were trapped forever in Ginnungagap, the vast gap between the fire and the mist. They might as well have been nowhere.

There was no sea and no sand, no grass nor rocks, no soil, no trees, no sky, no stars. There was no world, no heaven and no earth, at that time. The gap was nowhere: only an empty place waiting to be filled with life and with existence.

It was time for the creation of everything. Ve and Vili and Odin looked at each other and spoke of what was needful to do, there in the void of Ginnungagap. They spoke of the universe, and of life, and of the future.

Odin and Vili and Ve killed the giant Ymir. It had to be done. There was no other way to make the worlds. This was the beginning of all things, the death that made all life possible.

They stabbed the great giant. Blood gushed out from Ymir's corpse in unimaginable quantities; fountains of blood as salt as the sea and grey as the oceans gushed out in a flood so sudden, so powerful, and so deep that it swept away and drowned all the giants. (Only one giant, Bergelmir, Ymir's grandson, and his wife survived, by clambering on to a wooden box, which bore them like a boat. All the giants we see and we fear today are descended from them.)

Odin and his brothers made the soil from Ymir's flesh. Ymir's bones they piled up into mountains and cliffs.

Our rocks and pebbles, the sand and gravel you see: these were Ymir's teeth, and the fragments of bones that were broken and crushed by Odin and Vili and Ve in their battle with Ymir.

The seas that girdle the worlds: these were Ymir's blood and his sweat.

Look up into the sky: you are looking at the inside of Ymir's skull. The stars you see at night, the planets, all the comets and the shooting stars, these are the sparks that flew from the fires of Muspell. And the clouds you see by day? These were once Ymir's brains, and who knows what thoughts they are thinking, even now.

III

The world is a flat disk, and the sea encircles the perimeter. Giants live at the edges of the world, beside the deepest seas.

To keep the giants at bay, Odin and Vili and Ve made a wall from Ymir's eyelashes and set it around the middle of the world. They called the place within the wall Midgard.

Midgard was empty. The lands were beautiful, but nobody walked the meadows or fished in the clear waters, nobody explored the rocky mountains or stared up at the clouds.

Odin and Vili and Ve knew that a world is not a world until it is inhabited. They wandered high and low, looking for people, and they found nothing. At last, on the rocky shingle at the edge of the sea, they found two logs, sea-tossed, that had floated there on the tides and been cast ashore.

The first log was a log of ash wood. The ash tree is resilient and handsome and its roots go deep. Its wood carves well and will not split or crack. Ash wood makes a good tool handle, or the shaft of a spear.

The second log they found, beside the first on the beach, so close to the first log they were almost touching, was a log of elm wood. The elm tree is graceful, but its wood is hard enough to be made into the toughest planks and beams; you can build a fine home or a hall from elm wood.

The gods took the two logs. They set the logs so they were upright on the sand, the height of people. Odin held them, and one by one he breathed life into them. No longer were they dead logs on a beach: now they were alive.

Vili gave them will; he gave them intelligence and drive. Now they could move, and they could want.

Ve carved the logs. He gave them the shape of people. He carved their ears, that they might hear, and their eyes, that they might see, and lips, that they might speak.

The two logs stood on the beach, two naked people. Ve had carved one with male genitals, the other he had carved female.

The three brothers made clothes for the woman and the man, to cover themselves and to keep them warm, in the chilly sea spray on the beach at the edge of the world.

Last of all they gave the two people they had made names: the man they called Ask, or Ash Tree; the woman they called Embla, or Elm.

Ask and Embla were the father and the mother of all of us: every human being owes its life to its parents and their parents and their parents before them. Go far enough back, and the ancestors of each of us were Ask and Embla.

Embla and Ask stayed in Midgard, safe behind the wall the gods had made from Ymir's eyelashes. In Midgard they would make their homes, protected from giants and monsters and all the dangers that wait in the wastes. In Midgard they could raise their children in peace.

That is why Odin is called the all-father. Because he was the father of the gods, and because he breathed the breath of life into our grandparents' grandparents' grandparents. Whether we are gods or mortals, Odin is the father of us all.

YGGDRASIL
AND THE
NINE WORLDS

The ash tree Yggdrasil is a mighty ash tree, the most perfect and beautiful of all trees: also the largest. It grows between the nine worlds and joins them, each to each. It is the biggest of all the trees there are, and the finest. The tops of its branches are above the sky.

It is so large that the roots of the ash are in three worlds, and it is fed by three wells.

The first root, and the deepest, goes into the underworld, to Niflheim, the place that existed before other places. In the centre of the dark world is the ever-churning spring, Hvergelmir, so loud it sounds like a roaring kettle. The dragon Nidhogg lives in these waters, and it is always gnawing at the root from below.

The second root goes to the realm of the frost giants, to the well that belongs to Mimir.

There is an eagle who waits at the highest branches of the world-tree and who knows many things, and a hawk, who perches between the eagle's eyes.

A squirrel, Ratatosk, lives in the branches of the world-tree. It takes gossip and messages from Nidhogg, the dread corpse-eater, to the eagle and back again. The squirrel tells lies to both of them, and takes joy in provoking anger.

There are four stags who graze on the huge branches of the world-tree, devouring the foliage and the bark. There are uncountable snakes at the base of the tree, biting at the roots.

The world-tree can be climbed. It is from this tree that Odin hanged himself in sacrifice, making the world-tree a gallows and himself the gallows god.

The gods do not climb the world-tree. They travel between the worlds using Bifrost, the rainbow bridge. Only the gods can travel on the rainbow; it would burn the feet of any frost giants or trolls who attempted to clamber up it to reach Asgard.

These are the nine worlds:

Asgard, the home of the Aesir. This is where Odin makes his home.

Alfheim, where the light elves live. The light elves are as beautiful as the sun or the stars.

Nidavellir, which is sometimes called Svartalfheim, where the dwarfs (who are also known as dark elves) live beneath the mountains and build their remarkable creations.

Midgard, which is the world of women and men, the world in which we make our home.

Jotunheim, where the frost giants and the mountain giants wander and live and have their halls.

Vanaheim, where the Vanir live. The Aesir and the Vanir are gods, united by peace treaties, and many Vanir gods live in Asgard, with the Aesir.

Niflheim, the dark mist world.

Muspell, the world of flame, where Surtr waits.

And there is the place named after its ruler: Hel, where the dead go who did not die bravely in battle.

The last root of the world-tree goes to a spring in the home of the gods, to Asgard, where the Aesir make their home. Each day the gods hold their council here, and it is here they will gather in the last days of the world, before they set out for the final battle of Ragnarok. It is called the well of Urd.

There are three sisters, the norns, who are wise maidens. They tend the well, and make sure that the roots of Yggdrasil are covered with mud and cared for. The well belongs to Urd; she is fate, and destiny. She is your past. With her are Verdandi—her name means "becoming"—and hers is the present, and Skuld, whose name means "that which is intended", and her domain is the future.

The norns will decide what happens in your life. There are other norns, not just those three. Giant norns and elf norns, dwarf norns and Vanir norns, good norns and bad, and what your fate will be is decided by them. Some norns give people good lives, and others give us hard lives, or short lives, or twisted lives.

They will shape your fate, there at Urd's well.

MIMIR'S HEAD AND ODIN'S EYE

In Jotunheim, the home of the giants, is Mimir's well. It bubbles up from deep in the ground, and it feeds Yggdrasil, the world-tree. Mimir, the wise one, the guardian of memory, knows many things. His well is wisdom, and when the world was young he would drink every morning from the well, by dipping the horn known as the Gjallerhorn into the water and draining it.

Long, long ago, when the worlds were young, Odin put on his long cloak and his hat, and in the guise of a wanderer he travelled through the land of the giants, risking his life to get to Mimir, to seek wisdom.

"One drink from the water of your well, Uncle Mimir," said Odin. "That is all I ask for."

Mimir shook his head. Nobody drank from the well but Mimir himself. He said nothing: seldom do those who are silent make mistakes.

"I am your nephew," said Odin. "My mother, Bestla, was your sister."

"That is not enough," said Mimir.

"One drink. With a drink from your well, Mimir, I will be wise. Name your price."

"Your eye is my price," said Mimir. "Your eye in the pool."

Odin did not ask if he was joking. The journey through giant country to get to Mimir's well had been long and dangerous. Odin had been willing to risk his life to get there. He was willing to do more than that for the wisdom he sought.

Odin's face was set.

"Give me a knife," was all he said.

After he had done what was needful, he placed his eye carefully in the pool. It stared up at him through the water. Odin filled the Gjallerhorn with water from Mimir's pool, and he lifted it to his lips. The water was cold. He drained it down. Wisdom flooded into him. He saw farther and more clearly with his one eye than he ever had with two.

Thereafter Odin was given other names: Blindr, they called him, the blind god, and Hoarr, the one-eyed, and Baleyg, the flaming-eyed one.

Odin's eye remains in Mimir's well, preserved by the waters that feed the world ash, seeing nothing, seeing everything.

Time passed. When the war between the Aesir and the Vanir was ending and they were exchanging warriors and chiefs, Odin sent Mimir to the Vanir as an adviser to the Aesir god Hoenir, who would be the new chief of the Vanir.

Hoenir was tall and good-looking, and he looked like a king. When Mimir was with him to advise him, Hoenir also spoke like a king and made wise decisions. But when Mimir was not with him, Hoenir seemed unable to come to a decision, and the Vanir soon tired of this. They took their revenge, not on Hoenir but on Mimir: they cut off Mimir's head and sent it to Odin.

Odin was not angry. He rubbed Mimir's head with certain herbs to prevent it from rotting, and he chanted charms and incantations over it, for he did not wish Mimir's knowledge to be lost. Soon enough Mimir opened his eyes and spoke to him. Mimir's advice was good, as it was always good.

Odin took Mimir's head back to the well beneath the world-tree, and he placed it there, beside his eye, in the waters of knowledge of the future and of the past.

Odin gave the Gjallerhorn to Heimdall, watchman of the gods. On the day the Gjallerhorn is blown, it will wake the gods, no matter where they are, no matter how deeply they sleep.

Heimdall will blow the Gjallerhorn only once, at the end of all things, at Ragnarok.

THE TREASURES

OF THE GODS

I

Thor's wife was the beautiful Sif. She was of the Aesir. Thor loved her for herself, and for her blue eyes and her pale skin, her red lips and her smile, and he loved her long, long hair, the colour of a field of barley at the end of summer.

Thor woke, and stared at sleeping Sif. He scratched his beard. Then he tapped his wife with a huge hand. "What happened to you?" he asked.

She opened her eyes, the colour of the summer sky. "What are you talking about?" she asked, and then she moved her head and looked puzzled. Her fingers reached up to her bare pink scalp and touched it, exploring it tentatively. She looked at Thor, horrified.

"My hair," was all she said.

Thor nodded. "It's gone," he said. "He has left you bald."

"He?" asked Sif.

Thor said nothing. He strapped on his belt of power, Megingjord, which doubled his enormous strength. "Loki," he said. "Loki has done this."

"Why do you say that?" said Sif, touching her bald head frantically, as if the fluttering touch of her fingers would make her hair return.

"Because," said Thor, "when something goes wrong, the first thing I always think is, it is Loki's fault. It saves a lot of time."

Thor found Loki's door locked, so he pushed through it, leaving it in pieces. He picked Loki up and said only, "Why?"

"Why what?" Loki's face was the picture of perfect innocence.

"Sif's hair. My wife's golden hair. It was so beautiful. Why did you cut it off?"

A hundred expressions chased each other across Loki's face: cunning and shiftiness, truculence and confusion. Thor shook Loki hard. Loki looked down and did his best to appear ashamed. "It was funny. I was drunk."

Thor's brow lowered. "Sif's hair was her glory. People will think that her head was shaved for punishment. That she did something she should not have done, did it with someone she should not have."

"Well, yes. There is that," said Loki. "They *will* probably think that. And unfortunately, given that I took her hair from the roots, she will go through the rest of her life completely bald . . ."

"No, she won't." Thor looked up at Loki, whom he was now holding far above his head, with a face like thunder.

"I am afraid she will. But there are always hats and scarves . . ."

"She won't go through life bald," said Thor. "Because, Loki Laufey's son, if you do not put her hair back right now, I am going to break every single bone in your body. Each and every one of them. And if her hair does not grow properly, I will come back and break every bone in your body again. And again. If I do it every day, I'll soon get really good at it," he carried on, sounding slightly more cheerful.

"No!" said Loki. "I can't put her hair back. It doesn't work like that."

"Today," mused Thor, "it will probably take me about an hour to break every bone in your body. But I bet that with practice I could get it down to about fifteen minutes. It will be interesting to find out." He started to break his first bone.

"Dwarfs!" shrieked Loki.

"Pardon?"

"Dwarfs! They can make anything. They could make golden hair for Sif, hair that would bond with her scalp and grow normally, perfect golden hair. They could do it. I swear they could."

"Then," said Thor, "you had better go and talk to them." And he dropped Loki from high above his head on to the floor.

Loki clambered to his feet and hurried away before Thor could break any more bones.

He put on his shoes that let him travel through the sky, and he went to Svartalfheim, where the dwarfs have their workshops. The most ingenious craftsmen of them all, he decided, were the three dwarfs known as the sons of Ivaldi.

Loki went to their underground forge. "Hello, sons of Ivaldi. I have asked around, and people here tell me that Brokk and Eitri, his brother, are the greatest dwarf craftsmen there are or have ever been," said Loki.

"No," said one of the sons of Ivaldi. "It's us. We are the greatest craftsmen there are."

"I am assured that Brokk and Eitri can make treasures as good as those you can."

"Lies!" said the tallest of the sons of Ivaldi. "I wouldn't trust those fumble-fingered incompetents to shoe a horse."

The smallest and the wisest of the sons of Ivaldi simply shrugged. "Whatever they make, we could do better."

"I hear that they've challenged you," said Loki. "Three treasures. The gods of the Aesir will judge who made the best treasure. Oh, and by the way, one of the treasures you make needs to be hair. Ever-growing perfect golden hair."

"We can do that," said one of the sons of Ivaldi. Even Loki could barely tell them apart.

Loki went across the mountain to see the dwarf called Brokk, at the workshop he shared with his brother, Eitri. "Ivaldi's sons are making three treasures as gifts for the gods of Asgard," said Loki. "The gods are going to judge the treasures. Ivaldi's sons want me to tell you that they are certain you and your brother Eitri can't make anything as good as they can. They called you 'fumble-fingered incompetents'."

Brokk was no fool. "This smells extremely fishy to me, Loki," he said. "Are you sure this isn't your doing? Stirring up trouble between Eitri and me and Ivaldi's boys seems like the sort of thing you'd do."

Loki looked as guileless as he could, which was amazingly guileless. "Nothing to do with me," he said innocently. "I just thought you ought to know."

"And you have no personal stake in this?" asked Brokk.

"None whatsoever."

Brokk nodded and looked up at Loki. Brokk's brother, Eitri, was the great craftsman, but Brokk was the smarter of the two, and the more determined. "Well, then we'll be happy to take on the sons of Ivaldi in a test of skill, to be judged by the gods. Because I have no doubt that Eitri can forge better and craftier things than Ivaldi's lot. But let's make this personal, Loki. Eh?"

"What do you have in mind?" asked Loki.

"Your head," said Brokk. "If we win this contest, we get your head, Loki. There's lots of things going on in that head of yours, and I have no doubt that Eitri could make a wonderful device out of it. A thinking machine, perhaps. Or an inkwell."

Loki kept smiling, but he scowled on the inside. The day had started out so well. Still, he simply had to ensure that Eitri and Brokk lost the contest; the gods would still get six wonderful things from the dwarfs, and Sif would get her golden hair. He could do that. He was Loki.

"Of course," he said. "My head. No problem."

Across the mountain, the sons of Ivaldi were making their treasures. Loki was not worried about them. But he needed to make sure that Brokk and Eitri did not, could not possibly, win.

Brokk and Eitri entered the forge. It was dark in there, lit by the orange glow of burning charcoal. Eitri took a pigskin from a shelf and placed it into the forge. "I've been keeping this pigskin for something like this," he said.

Brokk just nodded.

"Right," said Eitri. "You work the bellows, Brokk. Just keep pumping them. I need this hot, and I need it consistently hot, otherwise it won't work. Pump. Pump."

Brokk began to pump the bellows, sending a stream of oxygen-rich air into the heart of the forge, heating everything up. He had done it many times before. Eitri watched until he was satisfied that it would all be to his liking.

Eitri left to work on his creation outside the forge. As he opened the door to go out, a large black insect flew in. It was not a horsefly and it was not a deerfly; it was bigger than either. It flew in and circled the room in a malicious way.

Brokk could hear the sound of Eitri's hammers outside the forge, and the sounds of filing and twisting, of shaping and banging.

The large black fly—it was the biggest, blackest fly you have ever seen—landed on the back of Brokk's hand.

Both of Brokk's hands were on the bellows. He did not stop pumping to swat at the fly. The fly bit Brokk, hard, on the back of the hand.

Brokk kept pumping.

The door opened, and Eitri came in and carefully pulled the work from the forge. It appeared to be a huge boar, with bristles of gleaming gold.

"Good work," said Eitri. "A fraction of a degree warmer or cooler and the whole thing would have been a waste of our time."

"Good work you too," said Brokk.

The black fly, up on the corner of the ceiling, seethed with resentment and irritation.

Eitri took a block of gold and placed it on the forge. "Right," he said. "This next one will impress them. When I call, start pumping the bellows, and whatever happens do not slow down, or speed up, or stop. There's fiddly work involved."

"Got it," said Brokk.

Eitri left the room and began to work. Brokk waited until he heard Eitri's call, and he started to pump the bellows.

The black fly circled the room thoughtfully, then landed on Brokk's neck. The insect stepped aside daintily to avoid a rivulet of sweat, for the air was hot and close in the forge. It bit Brokk's neck as hard as it could. Scarlet blood joined the sweat on Brokk's neck, but the dwarf did not stop pumping.

Eitri returned. He removed a white-hot arm-ring from the forge. He dropped it into the stone cooling pool in the forge to quench it. There was a cloud of steam as the arm-ring fell into the water. The ring cooled, moving rapidly to orange, to red hot, and then, as it cooled, to gold.

"It's called Draupnir," said Eitri.

"The dripper? That's a funny name for a ring," said Brokk.

"Not for this one," said Eitri, and he explained to Brokk what was so very special about the arm-ring.

"Now," said Eitri, "there's something I've had in mind to make for a very long time now. My masterwork. But it's even trickier than the other two. So what you have to do is—"

"Pump, and don't stop pumping?" said Brokk.

"That's right," said Eitri. "Even more than before. Do not change your pace, or the whole thing will be ruined." Eitri picked up an ingot of pig iron, bigger than any ingot that the black fly (who was Loki) had ever seen before, and he hefted it into the forge.

He left the room and called out to Brokk to begin pumping.

Brokk began to pump, and the sound of Eitri's hammers began as Eitri pulled and shaped and welded and joined.

Loki, in fly shape, decided that there was no more time

for subtlety. Eitri's masterpiece would be something that would impress the gods, and if the gods were impressed enough, then he would lose his head. Loki landed between Brokk's eyes and started to bite the dwarf's eyelids. The dwarf continued to pump, his eyes stinging. Loki bit deeper, harder, more desperately. Now blood ran from the dwarf's eyelids, into his eyes and down his face, blinding him.

Brokk squinted and shook his head, trying to dislodge the fly. He jerked his head from side to side. He contorted his mouth and tried blowing air up at the fly. It was no good. The fly continued to bite, and the dwarf could see nothing but blood. A sharp pain filled his head.

Brokk counted, and at the bottom of the downstroke he whipped one hand from the bellows and swiped at the fly, with such speed and such strength that Loki barely escaped with his life. Brokk grabbed the bellows once again and continued to pump.

"Enough!" called Eitri.

The black fly flew unsteadily about the room. Eitri opened the door, allowing the fly to escape.

Eitri looked at his brother with disappointment. Brokk's face was a mess of blood and sweat. "I don't know what you were playing at that time," said Eitri. "But you came close to ruining everything. The temperature was all over the place at the end. As it is, it's nowhere near as impressive as I'd hoped. We'll just have to see."

Loki, in Loki shape, strolled in through the open door. "So, all ready for the contest?" he asked.

"Brokk can go to Asgard and present my gifts to the gods and cut off your head," said Eitri. "I like it best here at my forge, making things."

Brokk stared at Loki through swollen eyelids. "I'm looking forward to cutting off your head," said Brokk. "It got personal."

II

In Asgard, three gods sat on their thrones: one-eyed Odin the all-father, red-bearded Thor of the thunders, and handsome Frey of the summer's harvest. They would be the judges.

Loki stood before them, beside the three almost identical sons of Ivaldi.

Brokk, black-bearded and brooding, was there alone, standing to one side, the things he had brought hidden beneath sheets.

"So," said Odin. "What are we judging?"

"Treasures," said Loki. "The sons of Ivaldi have made gifts for you, great Odin, and for Thor, and for Frey, and so have Eitri and Brokk. It is up to you to decide which of the six things is the finest treasure. I myself will show you the gifts made by the sons of Ivaldi."

He presented Odin with the spear called Gungnir. It was a beautiful spear, carved with intricate runes.

"It will penetrate anything, and when you throw it, it will always find its mark," said Loki. Odin had but one eye, after all, and sometimes his aim could be less than perfect. "And, just as important, an oath taken on this spear is unbreakable."

Odin hefted the spear. "It is very fine," was all he said.

"And here," said Loki proudly, "is a flowing head of golden hair. Made of real gold. It will attach itself to the head of the person who needs it and grow and behave in every way as if it were real hair. A hundred thousand strands of gold."

"I will test it," said Thor. "Sif, come here."

Sif rose and came to the front, her head covered. She removed her headscarf. The gods gasped when they saw Sif's naked head, bald and pink, and then she carefully placed the dwarfs' golden wig on her head and shook her hair. They watched as the base of the wig joined itself to her scalp, and then Sif stood in front of them even more radiant and beautiful than before.

"Impressive," said Thor. "Good job!"

Sif tossed her golden hair and walked out of the hall into the sunlight, to show her new hair to her friends.

The last of the sons of Ivaldi's remarkable gifts was small, and folded like cloth. This cloth Loki placed in front of Frey.

"What is it? It looks like a silk scarf," said Frey, unimpressed.

"It does," said Loki. "But if you unfold it, you will discover it is a ship, called *Skiðblaðnir*. It will always have a fair wind, wherever it goes. And although it is huge, the biggest ship you can imagine, it will fold up, as you see, like a cloth, so you can put it into your pouch."

Frey was impressed, and Loki was relieved. They were three excellent gifts.

Now it was Brokk's turn. His eyelids were red and swollen, and there was a huge insect bite on the side of his neck. Loki thought Brokk looked entirely too cocky, especially given the remarkable things Ivaldi's sons had made.

Brokk took the golden arm-ring and placed it in front of Odin on his high throne. "This arm-ring is called Draupnir," said Brokk. "Because every ninth night, eight gold arm-rings of equal beauty will drip from it. You can reward people with them, or store them, and your wealth will increase."

Odin examined the arm-ring, then pushed it on to his arm, up high on his biceps. It gleamed there. "It is very fine," he said.

Loki recalled that Odin had said the same thing about the spear.

Brokk walked over to Frey. He raised a cloth and revealed a huge boar with bristles made of gold.

"This is a boar my brother made for you, to pull your chariot," said Brokk. "It will race across the sky and over the sea, faster than the fastest horse. There will never be a night so dark that its golden bristles will not give light and let you see what you are doing. It will never tire, and will never fail you. It is called Gullinbursti, the golden-bristled one."

Frey looked impressed. Still, thought Loki, the magical

ship that folded up like a cloth was every bit as impressive as an unstoppable boar that shone in the dark. Loki's head was quite safe. And the last gift Brokk had to present was the one that Loki knew he had already managed to sabotage.

From beneath the cloth Brokk produced a hammer, and placed it in front of Thor.

Thor looked at it and sniffed.

"The handle is rather short," he said.

Brokk nodded. "Yes," he said. "That's my fault. I was working the bellows. But before you dismiss it, let me tell you about what makes this hammer unique. It's called Mjollnir, the lightning-maker. First of all, it's unbreakable— doesn't matter how hard you hit something with it, the hammer will always be undamaged."

Thor looked interested. He had already broken a great many weapons over the years, normally by hitting things with them.

"If you throw the hammer, it will never miss what you throw it at."

Thor looked even more interested. He had lost a number of otherwise excellent weapons by throwing them at things that irritated him and missing, and he had watched too many weapons he had thrown disappear into the distance, never to be seen again.

"No matter how hard or how far you throw it, it will always return to your hand."

Thor was now actually smiling. And the thunder god did not often smile.

"You can change the size of the hammer. It will grow, and it will also shrink down so small that if you wish, you can hide it inside your shirt."

Thor clapped his hands together in delight, and thunder echoed across Asgard.

"And yet, as you have observed," concluded Brokk sadly, "the handle of the hammer is indeed too short. This is my fault. I failed to keep the bellows blowing while my brother, Eitri, was forging it."

"The shortness of the handle is a minor, cosmetic problem," said Thor. "This hammer will protect us from the frost giants. This is the finest gift I have ever seen."

"It will protect Asgard. It will protect all of us," said Odin with approval.

"If I were a giant, I would be very afraid of Thor if he had that hammer," said Frey.

"Yes. It's an excellent hammer. But Thor, what about the hair? Sif's beautiful new golden hair!" asked Loki slightly desperately.

"What? Oh, yes. My wife has very nice hair," said Thor. "Now. Show me how to make the hammer grow and shrink, Brokk."

"Thor's hammer is better even than my wonderful spear and my excellent arm-ring," said Odin, nodding.

"The hammer is greater and more impressive than my ship and my boar," admitted Frey. "It will keep the gods of Asgard safe."

The gods clapped Brokk on the back and told him that

he and Eitri had made the finest gift that they had ever been given.

"Good to know," said Brokk. He turned to Loki. "So," said Brokk. "I get to cut off your head, Laufey's son, and take it back with me. Eitri will be so pleased. We can turn it into something useful."

"I . . . will ransom my head," said Loki. "I have treasures I can give you."

"Eitri and I already have all the treasure we need," said Brokk. "We *make* treasures. No, Loki. I want your head."

Loki thought for a moment, then said, "Then you can have it. If you can catch me." And Loki leapt high into the air and ran off, far above their heads. In moments he was gone.

Brokk looked at Thor. "Can you catch him?"

Thor shrugged. "I really shouldn't," he said. "But then, I would very much like to try out the hammer."

In moments Thor returned, holding Loki tightly. Loki was glaring with impotent fury.

The dwarf Brokk took out his knife. "Come here, Loki," he said. "I'm going to cut off your head."

"Of course," said Loki. "You can, of course, cut off my head. But—and I appeal to mighty Odin here—if you cut off any of my neck, you are violating the terms of our agreement, which promised you my head, and my head only."

Odin inclined his head. "Loki is right," he said. "You have no right to cut his neck."

Brokk was irritated. "But I can't cut off his head without cutting his neck," he said.

Loki looked pleased with himself. "You see," he said, "if people thought through the exactness of their words, they would not dare to take on Loki, the wisest, the cleverest, the trickiest, the most intelligent, the best-looking . . ."

Brokk whispered a suggestion to Odin. "That would be fair," agreed Odin.

Brokk produced a strip of leather and a knife. He wrapped the leather around Loki's mouth. Brokk tried to pierce the leather with the tip of the knifeblade.

"It's not working," said Brokk. "My knife isn't cutting you."

"I might have wisely arranged for protection from knifeblades," said Loki modestly. "Just in case the whole you-can't-cut-my-neck ploy did not work. I am afraid no knifeblade can cut me!"

Brokk grunted and produced an awl, a pointed spike used in leatherwork, and he jabbed it through the leather, punching holes through Loki's lips. Then he took a strong thread and he sewed Loki's lips together with it.

Brokk walked away, leaving Loki with his mouth sewn up tight, unable to complain.

For Loki, the pain of being unable to talk hurt even more than the pain of having his lips stitched into the leather.

So now you know: that is how the gods got their

greatest treasures. It was Loki's fault. Even Thor's hammer was Loki's fault. That was the thing about Loki. You resented him even when you were at your most grateful, and you were grateful to him even when you hated him the most.

THE MASTER

BUILDER

Thor had gone to the east to fight trolls. Asgard was more peaceful without him, but it was also unprotected. This was in the early days, shortly after the treaty between the Aesir and the Vanir, when the gods were still making a home for themselves and Asgard was undefended.

"We cannot always rely on Thor," said Odin. "We need protection. Giants will come. Trolls will come."

"What do you propose?" asked Heimdall, the watchman of the gods.

"A wall," said Odin. "High enough to keep out frost giants. Thick enough that not even the strongest troll could batter its way through."

"Building such a wall," said Loki, "so high and so thick, would take us many years."

Odin nodded his agreement. "But still," he said, "we need a wall."

The next day a newcomer arrived in Asgard. He was a big man, dressed as a smith, and behind him trudged a horse—a stallion, huge and grey, with a broad back.

"They say you need a wall built," said the stranger.

"Go on," said Odin.

"I can build you a wall," said the stranger. "Build it so high that the tallest giant could not climb it, so thick that the strongest troll could not batter through it. I can build it so well, by placing stone upon stone, that not an ant could find space enough to crawl through it. I will build you a wall that will last for a thousand thousand years."

"Such a wall would take a very long time to build," said Loki.

"Not at all," said the stranger. "I can build it in three seasons. Tomorrow is the first day of winter. It would only take me a winter, a summer and another winter to build."

"And if you could do this," said Odin, "what would you ask in return?"

"I need little enough payment for what I am offering," said the man. "Only three things. First, I would like the beautiful goddess Freya's hand in marriage."

"That is not a little thing," said Odin. "And it would not surprise me if Freya had her own opinions about the matter. What are the other two things?"

The stranger grinned a cocky grin. "If I build your wall," he said, "I want the hand of Freya, and I also want the sun that shines in the sky by day, and I want the moon that gives us light at night. These three things are what the gods will give me if I build your wall."

The gods looked at Freya. She said nothing, but her lips were pressed together and her face was white with anger. Around her neck was the necklace of the Brisings, which shone like the Northern Lights as it brushed her skin, and her hair was banded in gold, which was almost as bright as the hair itself.

"Go and wait outside," said Odin to the stranger. The man walked away, not before asking where he could find food and water for his stallion, which was called Svadilfari, which means "one who makes an unlucky journey."

Odin rubbed his forehead. Then he turned and looked at all the gods.

"Well?" asked Odin.

The gods began to talk.

"Quiet!" shouted Odin. "One at a time!"

Each of the gods and the goddesses had an opinion, and every one of them was of the same opinion: that Freya, the sun and the moon were all too important and too valuable to be given to a stranger, even if he could build them the wall they needed in three seasons.

Freya had an additional opinion. She felt that the man should be beaten for his impertinence, then thrown out of Asgard and sent on his way.

"So," said Odin the all-father, "we are decided. We say no."

There was a dry cough from a corner of the hall. It was the kind of cough intended to attract attention, and the gods turned to see who had coughed. They found themselves looking at Loki, who stared back at them, and who smiled and held up a finger as if he had something important to divulge.

"It is worth my pointing out," he said, "that you are ignoring something huge."

"I do not think we have overlooked a single thing, troublemaker of the gods," said Freya tartly.

"You are all overlooking," he said, "that what this stranger is proposing to do is, to make no bones about it, quite impossible. There is no one alive who could build a wall so high and so thick as the one he described and have it finished in eighteen months. Not a giant or a god could do this, let alone a mortal man. I would stake my skin on it."

At this the gods all nodded and grunted and looked impressed. All of them except for Freya, and she looked angry. "You are fools," she said. "Especially you, Loki, because you think yourself clever."

"What he says he can do," said Loki, "is an impossible task. So I suggest this: we agree to his demands and to his price, but we set him stiff conditions—he may have no help building his wall, and instead of three seasons to build his wall, he has but one. If on the first day of summer any of the wall is unfinished—and it will be—then we pay him nothing at all."

"Why would he agree to that?" asked Heimdall.

"And what advantage would that give us over not having a wall at all?" asked Frey, Freya's brother.

Loki tried to suppress his impatience. *Were all the gods fools?* He began to explain, as if he were explaining to a small child. "The smith will begin to build his wall. He will not finish it. He will work for six months, unpaid, on a fool's errand. At the end of six months we will drive him away—we might even beat him for his presumption—and then we can use whatever he has done so far as the foundations of the wall that we will complete in the years to come. There is no risk to us of losing Freya, let alone the sun or moon."

"Why would he say yes to building it in a season?" asked Tyr, god of war.

"He may not say yes," said Loki. "But he seems arrogant and sure of himself, and not the kind to refuse a challenge."

All the gods grunted, and clapped Loki on the back, and told him that he was a very crafty fellow and it was a good thing that he was crafty and on their side, and now they would get their foundations built for nothing, and they congratulated each other on their intelligence and their bargaining ability.

Freya said nothing. She fingered her necklace of light, the gift of the Brisings. This was the same necklace that had been stolen from her by Loki in the form of a seal, when she was bathing, and that Heimdall had fought in seal form with Loki to return to her. She did not trust Loki. She did not care for the way this conversation had gone.

The gods called the builder into their hall.

He looked around at the gods. They all seemed in good

humour, grinning and nudging each other and smiling. Freya, however, did not smile.

"Well?" asked the builder.

"You asked for three seasons," said Loki. "We will give you one season, and one season only. Tomorrow is the first day of winter. If you are not finished on the first day of summer, you leave here, unpaid. But if you have finished building the wall, as high and as thick and as impregnable as we have agreed, then you will be given everything you have asked for: the moon, the sun and the beautiful Freya. You may have no help in building your wall from anyone; you must build this wall alone."

The stranger said nothing for some moments. He stared away into the distance and seemed to be weighing Loki's words and conditions. Then he looked at the gods, and he shrugged. "You have said I may have no outside help. I would like my horse, Svadilfari, to help me haul the stones here, the stones I will use to build the wall. I do not believe this to be an unreasonable request."

"It is not unreasonable," agreed Odin, and the other gods nodded and told each other that horses were good for hauling heavy stones.

They swore oaths then, the mightiest of oaths, the gods and the stranger, that neither side could betray the other. They swore on their weapons, and they swore on Draupnir, Odin's golden arm-ring, and they swore on Gungnir, Odin's spear, and an oath sworn on Gungnir was unbreakable.

The next morning, as the sun rose, the gods stood to watch the man work. He spat on his hands and he began to dig the trench into which the first stones would go.

"He digs deep," said Heimdall.

"He digs fast," said Frey, Freya's brother.

"Well, yes, obviously he is a mighty digger of ditches and trenches," said Loki grudgingly. "But imagine how many stones he will have to haul here from the mountains. It is one thing to dig a trench. It is another to haul stones many miles, unaided, and then to place them, one stone upon the next, so tightly fitted that not an ant could crawl between them, higher than the tallest giant, to make a wall."

Freya looked at Loki with disgust, but she said nothing.

When the sun set, the builder mounted his horse and set off for the mountains to gather his first rocks. The horse dragged an empty stone-boat behind it, a low sled that it pulled across the soft earth. The gods watched them leave. The moon was high and pale in the early winter sky.

"He will be back in a week," said Loki. "I am curious to see how many rocks that horse can haul. It looks strong."

The gods went to their feast hall then, and there was much merriment and laughter, but Freya did not laugh.

It snowed before dawn, a light dusting of snowflakes, a presentiment of the deep snows that would come further into the winter.

Heimdall, who saw everything approaching Asgard and who missed nothing, woke the gods in the darkness. They gathered by the trench the stranger had dug the previous day. In the gathering dawn they watched the builder, walking beside his horse, coming towards them.

The horse was steadily dragging a score of blocks of granite, so heavy that the sled made deep ruts in the black earth.

When the man saw the gods he waved and called good morning cheerfully. He pointed to the rising sun, and he winked at the gods. Then he unhitched his horse from the rocks and let it graze while he began to manhandle the first of the granite blocks into the trench he had already dug to receive it.

"The horse is indeed strong," said Balder, most beautiful of all the Aesir. "No normal horse should be able to drag rocks that heavy."

"It is stronger than we imagined," said Kvasir the wise.

"Ah," said Loki. "The horse will soon tire. This was its first day on the job. It will not be able to haul that many stones every night. And winter is coming. The snows will be deep and thick, the blizzards will be blinding, and the way to the mountain will be difficult. There is nothing to worry about. This is all going according to plan."

"I hate you so much," said Freya, who stood unsmiling beside Loki. She walked back to Asgard in the dawn and did not stay to watch the stranger build the foundations of his wall.

Each night the builder and the horse and the empty stone-boat left for the mountain. Each morning they returned, with the horse dragging another twenty blocks of granite, every block larger than the tallest man.

Each day the wall grew, and by evening it was bigger and more imposing than it had been before.

Odin called the gods to him.

"The wall is growing apace," he said. "And we swore an unbreakable oath, a ring-oath and a weapon-oath, that if he finishes building his wall in time, we will give him the sun and the moon and the hand in marriage of Freya the beautiful."

Kvasir the wise said, "No man can do what this master builder is doing. I suspect that he must be something other than a man."

"A giant," said Odin. "Perhaps."

"If only Thor were here," sighed Balder.

"Thor is hammering trolls, away in the east," said Odin. "And even if he were to return, our oaths are mighty and binding."

Loki tried to reassure them. "We are like old women, getting ourselves all worried about nothing. The builder cannot finish the wall before the first day of summer, even if he is the most powerful giant in the land. It is impossible."

"I wish Thor were here," said Heimdall. "He would know what to do."

The snows fell, but the deep snow did not stop the wall-builder, and it did not slow Svadilfari, his horse. The grey stallion pulled his sled, piled high with rocks, through snowdrifts and through blizzards, up steep hills and down again, through icy gorges.

The days began to get longer.

Dawn came earlier each morning. The snows began to melt, and the wet mud that was exposed was thick and heavy, the kind of mud that clings to your boots and drags you down.

"The horse will never be able to haul those rocks through the mud," said Loki. "They will sink, and he will lose his footing."

But Svadilfari was sure-footed and implacable, even in the thickest, wettest mud, and he hauled the rocks to Asgard, although the stone-boat was so heavy it cut deep gashes into the sides of the hills. Now the builder was hauling the rocks up hundreds of feet and manhandling each rock into place.

The mud dried and the spring flowers came out: yellow coltsfoot, and white wood anemones in profusion—and the wall being built around Asgard was a glorious, imposing thing. When it was finished it would be impregnable: no giant, no troll, no dwarf, no mortal would be able to breach that wall. And the stranger continued to build it with relentless good humour. He did not seem to care if it rained or it snowed, and neither did his horse. Each morning they would bring the rocks from the mountains; each day the builder would lay the granite blocks upon the previous layer.

Now it was the last day of winter, and the wall was all but completed.

The gods sat on their thrones in Asgard, and they spoke.

"The sun," said Balder. "We have given away the sun."

"We placed the moon in the sky in order to mark off the days and the weeks of the year," said Bragi, god of poetry, moodily. "Now there will be no moon."

"And Freya, what would we do without Freya?" asked Tyr.

"If this builder is actually a giant," said Freya, with ice in her voice, "then I will marry him and follow him back to Jotunheim, and it will be interesting to see whom I hate more, him for taking me away or all of you for giving me to him."

"Now, don't be like that," began Loki, but Freya interrupted him and said, "If this giant does take me, and the sun and the moon, then I ask only one thing from the gods of Asgard."

"Name it," said Odin all-father, who had said nothing until now.

"I would like to see whoever caused this calamity killed before I go," said Freya. "I think it only fair. If I am to go into the land of the frost giants, if the moon and the sun are to be plucked from the sky and the world plunged into eternal darkness, then the life of the one who got us to this point should be forfeit."

"Ah," said Loki. "The apportioning of blame is so difficult. Who remembers exactly who suggested what? As

I recall, all the gods share equally in this unfortunate mistake. We all suggested it, we all agreed to it—"

"*You* suggested it," said Freya. "*You* talked these idiots into it. And I will see you dead before I leave Asgard."

"We all—" began Loki, but he saw the expressions on the faces of all the gods in that hall, and he fell silent.

"Loki son of Laufey," said Odin, "this is the result of your poor counsel."

"And it was as bad as all your other advice," said Balder. Loki shot him a resentful glance.

"We need the builder to lose his wager," said Odin. "Without violating the oath. He must fail."

"I don't know what you expect me to do about it," said Loki.

"I do not expect anything from you," said Odin. "But if this builder succeeds in finishing his wall by the end of tomorrow, then your death will be painful, and long, and a bad and shameful death at that."

Loki looked from one god to the next, and in each of their faces he saw his death, saw anger and resentment. He did not see mercy or forgiveness.

It would be a bad death indeed. But what were the alternatives? What could he do? He did not dare to attack the builder. On the other hand . . .

Loki nodded. "Leave it to me."

He walked from the hall, and none of the gods tried to stop him.

The builder finished placing his load of stones on the

wall. Tomorrow, on the first day of summer, as the sun was setting, he would finish his wall, and then he would leave Asgard with his wages. Only twenty more granite blocks to go. He clambered down the rough wooden scaffolding and whistled for his horse.

Svadilfari was grazing, as he normally was, in the long grass at the edge of the forest, almost half a mile from the wall, but he always came when his master whistled.

The builder grabbed the ropes that attached to the empty stone-boat and prepared to hitch it to his great grey horse. The sun was low in the sky, but it would not set for several hours, and the disc of the moon was pale, but it was there, high in the heavens, as well. Soon both of them would be his, the greater light and the lesser, and Freya the lady, who was more beautiful than either the sun or the moon. But the builder would not count his winnings before they were in his hands. He had worked so hard, and so long, for all the winter . . .

He whistled for the horse again. Odd—he had never needed to whistle twice. He could see Svadilfari now, shaking his head and almost prancing in the wildflowers of the spring meadow. The horse would take a step forward and then a step back, as if he could scent something enticing in the warm air of the spring evening but could not tell what the scent was.

"Svadilfari!" called the builder, and the stallion pricked his ears up and moved into a swift canter across the meadow, heading for the builder.

The builder watched his horse head towards him, and he felt satisfied. The hoofbeats pounded across the meadow, doubling and redoubling with the echoes that bounced from the high grey granite wall, so for one moment the builder imagined that a whole herd of horses was coming towards him.

No, thought the builder, just one horse.

He shook his head and realised his mistake. Not one horse. Not one set of hoofbeats. *Two . . .*

The other horse was a chestnut mare. The builder knew she was a mare immediately—he did not have to look between her legs. Every line of her, every inch of her, everything about the chestnut was female. Svadilfari wheeled as he ran across the meadow, then he slowed, and reared, and neighed loudly.

The chestnut mare ignored him. She stopped running, as if he were not there, and she put her head down and seemed to be cropping the grass as Svadilfari approached her, but when he was within a dozen yards she began to run from him, a canter that became a gallop, and the grey stallion ran behind her, trying to catch her, always a length or two behind, nipping at her rump and tail with his teeth, yet always missing.

They ran across the meadow together in the creamy golden light of the end of the day, the grey horse and the brown, sweat glistening on their flanks. It was almost a dance.

The builder clapped his hands loudly, and whistled,

and called Svadilfari's name, but the stallion ignored him.

The builder ran out, intending to catch the horse and bring him back to his senses, but the chestnut mare seemed almost to know what he intended, for she slowed and rubbed her ears and mane against the side of the stallion's head, and then ran, as if wolves were after her, towards the edge of the forest. Svadilfari ran after her, and in moments they both vanished into the shadows of the wood.

The builder cursed, and spat, and waited for his horse to reappear.

The shadows lengthened, and Svadilfari did not return.

The builder returned to his stone-boat. He looked into the woods. Then he spat on his hands, took hold of the ropes, and began to haul the stone-boat across the meadow of grasses and spring flowers, towards the mountain quarry.

He did not return at dawn. The sun was already high in the sky by the time the builder returned to Asgard, hauling the stone-boat behind him.

He had ten stone blocks on the stone-boat, all he could manage, and he was hauling and heaving the stone-boat and cursing the stones, but with each heave he got closer to the wall.

Beautiful Freya stood at the gateway, watching him.

"You have only ten stone blocks with you," she told

him. "You will need twice that many bricks to finish our wall."

The builder said nothing. He carried on hauling his blocks towards the unfinished gateway, his face a mask. There were no smiles, no winks—not any longer.

"Thor is returning from the east," Freya told him. "He will be with us soon."

The gods of Asgard came out to watch the builder as he hauled the rocks towards the wall. They joined Freya, stood about her protectively.

They watched, silently at first, and then they began to smile and to chuckle, and to call out questions.

"Hey!" shouted Balder. "You only get the sun if you finish that wall. Do you think you will be taking the sun home with you?"

"And the moon," said Bragi. "Such a pity you do not have your horse with you. He could have carried all the rocks you need."

And the gods laughed.

The builder let go of the stone-boat then. He faced the gods. "You cheated!" he said, and his face was scarlet with exertion and with anger.

"We have not cheated," said Odin. "No more than you have cheated. Do you think we would have let you build our wall if we had known you were a giant?"

The builder picked up a rock one-handed and smashed it against another, breaking the granite block into two. He turned to the gods, half of the rock in each hand, and now he was twenty, thirty, fifty feet tall. His face twisted; he no longer looked like the stranger who had arrived in Asgard a season before, placid and even-tempered. Now his face looked like the granite face of a cliff, twisted and sculpted by anger and hatred.

"I am a mountain giant," he said. "And you gods are nothing but cheats and vile oath-breakers. If I still had my horse, I would be finishing your wall now. I would be taking the lovely Freya and the sun and the moon for my wages. And I would be leaving you here in the darkness and the cold, without even beauty to cheer you."

"No oath was broken," said Odin. "But no oath can protect you from us now."

The mountain giant roared with anger and ran towards the gods, a huge lump of granite in each hand as a club.

The gods stood aside, and only now the giant saw who was standing behind them. A huge god, red-bearded and muscular, wearing iron gauntlets and holding an iron hammer, which he swung, once. He let go of the hammer when it was pointing at the giant.

There was a flash of lightning from the clear skies, followed by the dull boom of thunder as the hammer left Thor's hand.

The mountain giant saw the hammer getting rapidly bigger as it came hurtling towards him, and then he saw nothing else, not ever again.

The gods finished building the wall themselves, although it took them many more weeks to cut and haul the last ten blocks from the quarries high in the mountains and drag them all the way back to Asgard and place them in position at the top of the gateway. They were not as well shaped or as well fitted as the blocks the master builder had shaped and placed himself.

There were those of the gods who felt that they should have let the giant get even closer to finishing the wall before Thor killed him. Thor said that he appreciated the gods having some fun ready for him, when he got home from the east.

Strangely, for it was most unlike him, Loki was not around to be praised for his part in luring away the horse Svadilfari. Nobody knew where he was, although there were those who spoke of a magnificent chestnut mare seen on the meadows beneath Asgard. Loki stayed away for the best part of a year, and when he showed up again, he was accompanied by a grey foal.

It was a beautiful foal, although it had eight legs instead of the usual four, and it followed Loki wherever he went, and nuzzled him, and treated Loki as if he were its mother. Which, of course, was the case.

The foal grew into a horse called Sleipnir, a huge grey stallion, the fastest and the strongest horse that ever there had been or ever there would be, a horse that could outrun the wind.

Loki presented Sleipnir to Odin as a gift, the best horse among gods and men.

Many people would admire Odin's horse, but only

a brave man would ever mention its parentage in Loki's presence, and nobody ever dared to allude to it twice. Loki would go out of his way to make your life unpleasant if he heard you talking about how he lured Svadilfari away from its master and how he rescued the gods from his own bad idea. Loki nursed his resentments.

And that is the story of how the gods got their wall.

THE CHILDREN

OF LOKI

Loki was handsome, and he knew it. People wanted to like him, they wanted to believe him, but he was undependable and self-centred at best, mischievous or evil at worst. He married a woman named Sigyn, who had been happy and beautiful when Loki courted and married her but now always looked like she was expecting bad news. She bore him a son, Narfi, and shortly afterwards another son, Vali.

Sometimes Loki would vanish for long periods and not return, and then Sigyn would look like she was expecting the very worst news of all, but always Loki would come back to her, looking shifty and guilty and also as if he were very proud of himself indeed.

Three times he went away, three times he—eventually— returned.

The third time Loki returned to Asgard, Odin called Loki to him.

"I have dreamed a dream," said the wise old one-eyed god. "You have children."

"I have a son, Narfi. A good boy, although I must confess that he does not always listen to his father, and another son, Vali, obedient and restrained."

"Not them. You have three other children, Loki. You have been sneaking off to spend your days and your nights in the land of the frost giants with Angrboda the giantess. And she has borne you three children. I have seen them in the eye of my mind as I sleep, and my visions tell me that they will be the greatest foes of the gods in the time that is to come."

Loki said nothing. He tried to look ashamed and succeeded simply in looking pleased with himself.

Odin called the gods to him, with Tyr and Thor at their head, and he told them that they would be journeying far into Jotunheim, to Giantland, to bring Loki's children to Asgard.

The gods travelled into the land of the giants, battling many dangers, until they reached Angrboda's keep. She was not expecting them, and she had left her children playing together in her great hall. The gods were shocked when they saw what Loki and Angrboda's children were, but that did not deter them. They seized the children, and they bound them, and they carried the oldest between them, tied to the stripped trunk of a pine tree, and they muzzled the second child with a muzzle made from knotted willow, and they put a rope around its neck as a leash, while the third child walked beside them, gloomy and disturbing.

Those on the right of the third child saw a beautiful

young girl, while those on the left tried not to look at her, for they saw a dead girl, her skin and flesh rotted black, walking in their midst.

"Have you noticed something?" Thor asked Tyr on the third day of their journey back through the land of the frost giants. They had camped for the night in a small clearing, and Tyr was scratching the furry neck of Loki's second child with his huge right hand.

"What?"

"They are not following us, the giants. Not even the creatures' mother has come after us. It's as if they *want* us to take Loki's children out of Jotunheim."

"That is foolish talk," said Tyr, but as he said it, even though the fire was warm, he shivered.

Two more days of hard travelling and they were in Odin's hall.

"These are the children of Loki," said Tyr shortly.

The first of Loki's children was tied to a pine tree and was now longer than the pine tree it was tied to. It was called Jormungundr, and it was a serpent. "It has grown many feet in the days we have carried it back," said Tyr.

Thor said, "Careful. It can spit burning black venom. It spat its poison at me, but it missed. That's why we tied its head to the tree like that."

"It is a child," said Odin. "It is still growing. We will send it where it can harm nobody."

Odin took the serpent to the shore of the sea that lies beyond all lands, the sea that circles Midgard, and there on the shore he freed Jormungundr, and watched it slither and slip beneath the waves and swim away in loops and curls.

Odin watched it with his one eye until it was lost on the horizon, and he wondered if he had done the right thing. He did not know. He had done as his dreams had told him, but dreams know more than they reveal, even to the wisest of the gods.

The serpent would grow beneath the grey waters of the world ocean, grow until it encircled the earth. Folk would call Jormungundr the Midgard serpent.

Odin returned to the great hall, and he ordered Loki's daughter to step forward.

He stared at the girl: on the right side of her face her cheek was pink and white, her eye was the green of Loki's eyes, her lips were full and carmine; on the left side of her face the skin was blotched and striated, swollen in the bruises of death, her sightless eye rotted and pale, her lipless mouth wizened and stretched over skull-brown teeth.

"What do they call you, girl?" asked the all-father.

"They call me Hel," she said, "if it pleases you, All-father."

"You are a polite child," said Odin. "I'll give you that."

Hel said nothing, only looked at him with her single green eye, sharp as an ice chip, and her pallid eye, dull and spoiled and dead, and he saw no fear in her.

"Are you alive?" he asked the girl. "Or are you a corpse?"

"I am only myself, Hel, daughter of Angrboda and of Loki," she said. "And I like the dead best of all. They are simple things, and they talk to me with respect. The living look at me with revulsion."

Odin contemplated the girl, and he remembered his dreams. Then Odin said, "This child will be the ruler of the deepest of the dark places, and ruler of the dead of all the nine worlds. She will be the queen of those poor souls who die in unworthy ways—of disease or of old age, of accidents or in childbirth. Warriors who die in battle will always come to us here in Valhalla. But the dead who die in other ways will be her folk, to attend her in her darkness."

For the first time since she had been taken from her mother, the girl Hel smiled, with half a mouth.

Odin took Hel down to the lightless world, and he showed her the immense hall in which she would receive her subjects, and watched as she named her possessions. "I will call my bowl Hunger," said Hel. She picked up a knife. "This is called Famine. And my bed is called Sickbed."

That was two of Loki's children with Angrboda dealt with, then. One in the ocean, one to the darkness beneath the earth. But what to do with the third?

When they had brought the third and smallest of Loki's children back from the land of the giants, it had been puppy-sized, and Tyr had scratched its neck and its head and played with it, removing its willow muzzle first.

It was a wolf cub, grey and black, with eyes the colour of dark amber.

The wolf cub ate its meat raw, but it spoke as a man would speak, in the language of men and the gods, and it was proud. The little beast was called Fenrir.

It too was growing fast. One day it was the size of a wolf, the next the size of a cave bear, then the size of a great elk.

The gods were intimidated by it, all except Tyr. He still played with it and romped with it, and he alone fed the wolf its meat each day. And each day the beast ate more than the day before, and each day it grew and it became fiercer and stronger.

Odin watched the wolf-child grow with foreboding, for in his dreams the wolf had been there at the end of everything, and the last things Odin had seen in any of his dreams of the future were the topaz eyes and the sharp white teeth of Fenris Wolf.

The gods had a council and resolved at that council that they would bind Fenrir.

They crafted heavy chains and shackles in the forges of the gods, and they carried the shackles to Fenrir.

"Here!" said the gods, as if suggesting a new game. "You have grown so fast, Fenrir. It is time to test your strength. We have here the heaviest chains and shackles. Do you think you can break them?"

"I think I can," said Fenris Wolf. "Bind me."

The gods wrapped the huge chains around Fenrir and

shackled his paws. He waited motionless while they did this. The gods smiled at each other as they chained the enormous wolf.

"Now," shouted Thor.

Fenrir strained and stretched the muscles of his legs, and the chains snapped like dry twigs.

The great wolf howled to the moon, a howl of triumph and joy. "I broke your chains," he said. "Do not forget this."

"We will not forget," said the gods.

The next day Tyr went to take the wolf his meat. "I broke the fetters," said Fenrir. "I broke them easily."

"You did," said Tyr.

"Do you think they will test me again? I grow, and I grow stronger with every day."

"They will test you again. I would wager my right hand on it," said Tyr.

The wolf was still growing, and the gods were in the smithies, forging a new set of chains. Each link in the chains was too heavy for a normal man to lift. The metal of the chains was the strongest metal that the gods could find: iron from the earth mixed with iron that had fallen from the sky. They called these chains Dromi.

The gods hauled the chains to where Fenrir slept.

The wolf opened his eyes.

"Again?" he said.

"If you can escape from these chains," said the gods, "then your renown and your strength will be known to all the worlds. Glory will be yours. If chains like this cannot hold you, then your strength will be greater than that of any of the gods or the giants."

Fenrir nodded at this, and looked at the chains called Dromi, bigger than any chains had ever been, stronger than the strongest of bonds. "There is no glory without danger," said the wolf after some moments. "I believe I can break these bindings. Chain me up."

They chained him.

The great wolf stretched and strained, but the chains held. The gods looked at each other, and there was the beginning of triumph in their eyes, but now the huge wolf began to twist and to writhe, to kick out his legs and strain in every muscle and every sinew. His eyes flashed and his teeth flashed and his jaws foamed.

He growled as he writhed. He struggled with all his might.

The gods moved back involuntarily, and it was good that they did so, for the chains fractured and then broke with such violence that the pieces were thrown far into the air, and for years to come the gods would find lumps of shattered shackles embedded in the sides of huge trees or the side of a mountain.

"Yes!" shouted Fenrir, and howled in his victory like a wolf and like a man.

The gods who had watched the struggle did not seem, the wolf observed, to delight in his victory. Not even Tyr. Fenrir, Loki's child, brooded on this, and on other matters.

And Fenris Wolf grew huger and hungrier with each day that passed.

Odin brooded and he pondered and he thought. All the wisdom of Mimir's well was his, and the wisdom he had gained from hanging from the world-tree, a sacrifice to himself. At last he called the light elf Skirnir, Frey's messenger, to his side, and he described the chain called Gleipnir. Skirnir rode his horse across the rainbow bridge to Svartalfheim, with instructions to the dwarfs for how to create a chain unlike anything ever made before.

The dwarfs listened to Skirnir describe the commission, and they shivered, and they named their price. Skirnir agreed, as he had been instructed to do by Odin, although the dwarfs' price was high. The dwarfs gathered the ingredients they would need to make Gleipnir.

These were the six things the dwarfs gathered:

For firstly, the footsteps of a cat.
For secondly, the beard of a woman.
For thirdly, the roots of a mountain.
For fourthly, the sinews of a bear.
For fifthly, the breath of a fish.
For sixth and lastly, the spittle of a bird.

Each of these things was used to make Gleipnir. (You say you have not seen these things? Of course you have not. The dwarfs used them in their crafting.)

When the dwarfs had finished their crafting, they gave Skirnir a wooden box. Inside the box was something that looked like a long silken ribbon, smooth and soft to the touch. It was almost transparent, and weighed next to nothing.

Skirnir rode back to Asgard with his box at his side. He arrived late in the evening, after the sun had set. He showed the gods what he had brought back from the workshop of the dwarfs, and they were amazed to see it.

The gods went together to the shores of the Black Lake, and they called Fenrir by name. He came at a run, as a dog will come when it is called, and the gods marvelled to see how big he was and how powerful.

"What's happening?" asked the wolf.

"We have obtained the strongest bond of all," they told him. "Not even you will be able to break it."

The wolf puffed himself up. "I can burst any chains," he told them proudly.

Odin opened his hand to display Gleipnir. It shimmered in the moonlight.

"That?" said the wolf. "That is nothing."

The gods pulled on it to show him how strong it was. "We cannot break it," they told him.

The wolf squinted at the silken band that they held between them, glimmering like a snail's trail or the moonlight on the waves, and he turned away, uninterested.

"No," he said. "Bring me real chains, real fetters, heavy ones, huge ones, and let me show my strength."

"This is Gleipnir," said Odin. "It is stronger than any chains or fetters. Are you scared, Fenrir?"

"Scared? Not at all. But what happens if I break a thin ribbon like that? Do you think I will get renown and fame? That people will gather together and say, 'Do you know how strong and powerful Fenris Wolf is? He is so powerful he broke a silken ribbon!' There will be no glory for me in breaking Gleipnir."

"You are scared," said Odin.

The great beast sniffed the air. "I scent treachery and trickery," said the wolf, his amber eyes flashing in the moonlight. "And although I think your Gleipnir may only be a ribbon, I will not consent to be tied up by it."

"You? You who broke the strongest, biggest chains there ever were? You are scared by this band?" said Thor.

"I am scared of nothing," growled the wolf. "I think it is rather that you little creatures are scared of me."

Odin scratched his bearded chin. "You are not stupid, Fenrir. There is no treachery here. But I understand your reluctance. It would take a brave warrior to consent to be tied up with bonds he could not break. I assure you, as the father of the gods, that if you cannot break a band like this—a veritable silken ribbon, as you say—then we gods will have no reason to be afraid of you, and we will set you free and let you go your own way."

A long growl, from the wolf. "You lie, All-father. You lie in the way that some folk breathe. If you were to tie me up in bonds I could not escape from, then I do not believe you would free me. I think you would leave me here. I think you plan to abandon me and to betray me. I do not consent to have that ribbon placed on me."

"Fine words, and brave words," said Odin. "Words to cover your fear at being proved a coward, Fenris Wolf.

You are afraid to be tied with this silken ribbon. No need for more explanations."

The wolf's tongue lolled from his mouth, and he laughed then, showing sharp teeth each the size of a man's arm. "Rather than question my courage, I challenge you to prove there is no treachery planned. You can tie me up if one of you will place his hand in my mouth. I will gently close my teeth upon it, but I will not bite down. If there is no treachery afoot, I will open my mouth when I have escaped the ribbon, or when you have freed me, and his hand will be unharmed. There. I swear, if I have a hand in my mouth, you can tie me with your ribbon. So. Whose hand will it be?"

The gods looked at each other. Balder looked at Thor, Heimdall looked at Odin, Hoenir looked at Frey, but none of them made a move. Then Tyr, Odin's son, sighed, and stepped forward and raised his right hand.

"I will put my hand in your mouth, Fenrir," said Tyr.

Fenrir lay on his side, and Tyr put his right hand into Fenrir's mouth, just as he had done when Fenrir was a puppy and they had played together. Fenrir closed his teeth gently until they held Tyr's hand at the wrist without breaking the skin, and he closed his eyes.

The gods bound him with Gleipnir. A shimmering snail's trail wrapped the enormous wolf, tying his legs, rendering him immobile.

"There," said Odin. "Now, Fenris Wolf, break your bonds. Show us all how powerful you are."

The wolf stretched and struggled; it pushed and strained every nerve and muscle to snap the ribbon that bound it. But with every struggle the task seemed harder and with every strain the glimmering ribbon became stronger.

At first the gods sniggered. Then the gods chuckled. Finally, when they were certain that the beast had been immobilised and that they were in no danger, the gods laughed.

Only Tyr was silent. He did not laugh. He could feel the sharpness of Fenris Wolf's teeth against his wrist, the wetness and warmth of Fenris Wolf's tongue against his palm and his fingers.

Fenrir stopped struggling. He lay there unmoving. If the gods were going to free him, they would do it now.

But the gods only laughed the harder. Thor's booming guffaws, each louder than a thunderclap, mingled with Odin's dry laughter, with Balder's bell-like laughter . . .

Fenrir looked at Tyr. Tyr looked at him bravely. Then Tyr closed his eyes and nodded. "Do it," he whispered.

Fenrir bit down on Tyr's wrist.

Tyr made no sound. He simply wrapped his left hand around the stump of his right and squeezed it as hard as he could, to slow the spurt of blood to an ooze.

Fenrir watched the gods take one end of Gleipnir and thread it through a stone as big as a mountain and fasten it under the ground. Then he watched as they took another rock and used it to hammer the stone deeper into the ground than the deepest ocean.

"Treacherous Odin!" called the wolf. "If you had not lied to me, I would have been a friend to the gods. But your fear has betrayed you. I will kill you, Father of the Gods. I will wait until the end of all things, and I will eat the sun and I will eat the moon. But I will take the most pleasure in killing you."

The gods were careful not to get within reach of Fenrir's jaws, but as they were driving the rock deeper, Fenrir twisted and snapped at them. The god nearest him, with presence of mind, thrust his sword into the roof of Fenris Wolf's mouth. The hilt of the sword jammed in the wolf's lower jaw, wedging the jaw open and preventing it from ever closing.

The wolf growled inarticulately, and saliva poured from its mouth, forming a river. If you did not know it was a wolf, you might have thought it a small mountain, with a river flowing from a cave mouth.

The gods left that place where the river of saliva flowed down into the dark lake, and they did not speak, but once they were far enough away they laughed some more, and clapped each other on the back, and smiled the huge smiles of those who believe they have done something very clever indeed.

Tyr did not smile and he did not laugh. He bound the stump of his wrist tightly with a cloth, and he walked beside the gods back to Asgard, and he kept his own counsel.

These, then, were the children of Loki.

FREYA'S UNUSUAL
WEDDING

Thor, god of thunder, mightiest of all the Aesir, the strongest, the bravest, the most valiant in battle, was not entirely awake yet, but he had the feeling that something was wrong. He reached out a hand for his hammer, which he always kept within reach while he slept.

He fumbled around with his eyes closed. He groped about, reaching for the comfortable and familiar shaft of his hammer.

No hammer.

Thor opened his eyes. He sat up. He stood up. He walked around the room.

There was no hammer anywhere. His hammer was gone.

Thor's hammer was called Mjollnir. It had been made for Thor by the dwarfs Brokk and Eitri. It was one of the treasures of the gods. If Thor hit anything with it, that thing would be destroyed. If he threw the hammer at something, the hammer would never miss its target, and would always fly back through the air and return to his hand. He could shrink the hammer down and hide it inside his shirt, and he could make it grow again. It was a perfect hammer in all things except one: it was slightly too short in the handle, which meant that Thor had to swing it one-handed.

The hammer kept the gods of Asgard safe from all the dangers that menaced them and the world. Frost giants and ogres, trolls and monsters of every kind, all were frightened of Thor's hammer.

Thor loved his hammer. And his hammer simply was not there.

There were things Thor did when something went wrong. The first thing he did was ask himself if what had happened was Loki's fault. Thor pondered. He did not believe that even Loki would have dared to steal his hammer. So he did the next thing he did when something went wrong, and he went to ask Loki for advice.

Loki was crafty. Loki would tell him what to do.

"Don't tell anyone," said Thor to Loki, "but the hammer of the gods has been stolen."

"That," said Loki, making a face, "is not good news. Let me see what I can find out."

Loki went to Freya's hall. Freya was the most beautiful of all the gods. Her golden hair tumbled about her shoulders, and it glinted in the morning light. Freya's two cats prowled the room, eager to pull her chariot. Around her neck, as golden and shining as her hair, glittered the necklace of the Brisings, made for Freya by dwarfs far underground.

"I'd like to borrow your feathered cloak," said Loki. "The one that lets you fly."

"Absolutely not," said Freya. "That cloak is the most valuable thing I possess. It's more valuable than gold. I'm not having you wearing it and going around and making mischief."

"Thor's hammer has been stolen," said Loki. "I need to find it."

"I'll get you the cloak," said Freya.

Loki put on the feathered cloak and he took to the air, in falcon shape. He flew beyond Asgard. He flew deep into the land of the giants, looking for something unusual.

Beneath him, Loki saw a huge grave mound, and sitting on it, plaiting a dog collar, was the hugest, ugliest ogre of a giant he had ever seen. When the ogre saw Loki in falcon shape, he grinned a sharp-toothed grin and waved.

"What's up with the Aesir, Loki? What's the news from the elves? And why have you come alone into the land of the giants?"

Loki landed beside the ogre. "There's nothing but bad news from Asgard, and nothing but bad news from the elves."

"Really?" said the ogre, and he chuckled to himself, as if he were extremely pleased with something he had done and thought himself remarkably clever. Loki recognised that sort of chuckle. Sometimes he did it himself.

"Thor's hammer is missing," said Loki. "Would you know anything about that?"

The ogre scratched his armpit, and he chuckled once more. "I might," he admitted. Then he said, "How's Freya? Is she as beautiful as they say?"

"If you like that sort of thing," said Loki.

"Oh, I do," said the ogre. "I *do*."

There was another uncomfortable silence. The ogre put the dog collar down on a pile of dog collars and began to plait another.

"I have Thor's hammer," the ogre told Loki. "I've hidden it so deep beneath the earth that nobody could ever find it, not even Odin. I am the only one who could bring it up again. And I will return it to Thor if you bring me what I want."

"I can ransom the hammer," said Loki. "I can bring you gold and amber, I can bring you treasures beyond counting—"

"Don't want them," said the ogre. "I want to marry Freya. Bring her here in eight days from now. I'll return the hammer of the gods as a bride-gift on Freya's wedding night."

"Who are you?" asked Loki.

The ogre grinned and showed his crooked teeth. "Why, Loki, son of Laufey, I am Thrym, lord of the ogres."

"I have no doubt that we can come to an arrangement, great Thrym," said Loki. He drew Freya's feathered cloak around him, then stretched his arms and took to the skies.

Beneath Loki the world seemed very small: he looked down at the trees and the mountains, tiny as children's playthings, and the problems of the gods seemed a small thing also.

Thor was waiting for him in the court of the gods, and before Loki had even landed he found himself seized by Thor's huge hands. "Well? You know something. I can see it in your face. Tell me whatever you know, and tell it now. I don't trust you, Loki, and I want to know what you know right this moment, before you've had a chance to plot and to plan."

Loki, who plotted and planned as easily as other folk breathed in and out, smiled at Thor's anger and innocence. "Your hammer has been stolen by Thrym, lord of all the ogres," he said. "I have persuaded him to return it to you, but he demands a price."

"Fair enough," said Thor. "What's the price?"

"Freya's hand in marriage."

"He just wants her hand?" asked Thor hopefully. She had two hands, after all, and might be persuaded to give up one of them without too much of an argument. Tyr had, after all.

"All of her," said Loki. "He wants to marry her."

"Oh," said Thor. "She won't like that. Well, you can tell her the news. You're better at persuading people to do things than I am when I'm not holding my hammer."

They went together to Freya's court once more.

"Here's your feathered cloak," said Loki.

"Thank you," said Freya. "Did you find out who stole Thor's hammer?"

"Thrym, lord of the ogres."

"I've heard of him. A nasty piece of work. What does he want for it?"

"You," said Loki. "He wants to marry you."

Freya nodded.

Thor was pleased that she seemed to have accepted the idea so easily. "Put on your bridal crown, Freya, and pack your things," he said. "You and Loki are going to the land of the giants. We need to get you married off to Thrym before he changes his mind. I want my hammer back."

Freya did not say anything.

Thor noticed that the ground was shaking, as were the walls. Freya's cats mewed and hissed, and they fled beneath a chest of furs and would not come out.

Freya's hands were squeezed into tight fists. The necklace of the Brisings tumbled from her neck to the floor. She did not appear to notice. She was staring at Thor and Loki as if they were the lowest, most unpleasant vermin she had ever seen.

Thor was almost relieved when Freya began to speak.

"What kind of person do you think I am?" she asked very quietly. "Do you think I'm that foolish? That disposable? That I'm someone who would actually marry an ogre just to get you out of trouble? If you two think that I am going to the land of the giants, that I'll put on a bridal crown and veil and submit to the touch and the . . . the *lust* of that ogre . . . that I'd marry him . . .

well . . ." She stopped talking. The walls shuddered once again, and Thor feared the entire building would fall upon them.

"Get out," said Freya. "What kind of woman do you think I am?"

"But. My hammer," said Thor.

"Shut up, Thor," said Loki.

Thor shut up. They left.

"She's very beautiful when she's angry," said Thor. "You can see why that ogre wants to marry her."

"Shut up, Thor," said Loki again.

They called a gathering of all the gods in the great hall. Every god and goddess was there except Freya, who declined to leave her house.

All day they talked, debated, and argued. There was no question that they needed to get Mjollnir back, but how? Each god and goddess made a suggestion, and each suggestion was shot down by Loki.

In the end only one god had not spoken: Heimdall, the far-seeing, who watches over the world. Not one thing happens that Heimdall does not see, and sometimes he sees events that have yet to occur in the world.

"Well?" said Loki. "What about you, Heimdall? Do you have any suggestions?"

"I do," said Heimdall. "But you won't like it."

Thor banged his fist down upon the table. "It does not matter whether or not we like it," he said. "We are gods! There is nothing that any of us gathered here would not do to get back Mjollnir, the hammer of the gods. Tell us your idea, and if it is a good idea, we will like it."

"You won't like it," said Heimdall.

"We will like it!" said Thor.

"Well, " said Heimdall, "I think we should dress Thor as a bride. Have him put on the necklace of the Brisings. Have him wear a bridal crown. Stuff his dress so he looks like a woman. Veil his face. We'll have him wear keys that jingle, as women do, drape him with jewels—"

"I don't like it!" said Thor. "People will think . . . well, for a start they'll think I dress up in women's clothes. Absolutely out of the question. I don't like it. I am definitely not going to be wearing a bridal veil. None of us like this idea, do we? Terrible, terrible idea. I've got a beard. I can't shave off my beard."

"Shut up, Thor," said Loki, son of Laufey. "It's an excellent idea. If you don't want the giants to invade Asgard, you will put on a wedding veil, which will hide your face—and your beard."

Odin the all-highest said, "It is indeed an excellent idea. Well done, Heimdall. We need the hammer back, and this is the best way. Goddesses, prepare Thor for his wedding night."

The goddesses brought him things to wear. Frigg and Fulla, Sif, Idunn and the rest, even Skadi, Freya's stepmother, came and helped to prepare him. They dressed him in the finest clothes, the kind a high-born goddess would wear to her wedding. Frigg went to see Freya and came back with the necklace of the Brisings, and she hung it about Thor's neck.

Sif, Thor's wife, hung her keys at Thor's side.

Idunn brought all her jewels, which she draped about Thor so that he glittered and gleamed in the candlelight, and she brought a hundred rings, of red gold and white gold, to go on Thor's fingers.

They covered his face with a veil, so that only his eyes could be seen, and Var, the goddess of marriage, placed a shining headdress upon Thor's head: a bridal crown, high and wide and beautiful.

"I'm not sure about the eyes," Var said. "They don't look very feminine."

"I should hope not," muttered Thor.

Var looked at Thor. "If I pull down the headdress, it will hide them, but he still has to be able to see."

"Do your best," said Loki. And then he said, "I'll be your maidservant and go with you to the land of the giants." Loki shifted his shape, and now he was, in voice and in appearance, a beautiful young serving woman. "There. How do I look?"

Thor muttered something under his breath, but it might have been a good thing that nobody could hear it.

Loki and Thor clambered into Thor's chariot, and the goats who pulled it, Snarler and Grinder, leapt into the skies, eager to be off. Mountains broke in half as they passed, and the earth burst into flame beneath them.

"I have a bad feeling about this," said Thor.

"Don't speak," said Loki in the form of a maiden. "Let me do all the talking. Can you remember that? If you speak, you may ruin everything."

Thor grunted.

They landed in the courtyard. Giant-sized jet-black oxen stood impassively. Each beast was larger than a house; the tips of their horns were capped with gold, and the courtyard stank with the sharp smell of their dung.

A booming voice could be heard from inside the huge high hall: "Move it, you fools! Spread clean straw on the benches! What do you think you're doing? Well, pick it up or cover it with straw, don't just leave it there to rot. This is Freya, the most beautiful creature in existence, Njord's daughter, who comes to us. She won't want to see something like that."

There was a path made of fresh straw through the courtyard, and after leaving their chariot, the disguised Thor and the serving maiden who was Loki walked across the straw, lifting their skirts so they did not drag in the muck.

A giant woman was waiting for them. She introduced herself as Thrym's sister, and she reached down and pinched Loki's pretty cheek between her fingertips, and she prodded Thor with one sharp fingernail. "So this is the most beautiful woman in the world? Doesn't look much to me. And when she picked up her skirts, it seemed to me that her ankles were as thick as small tree trunks."

"A trick of the light. She is the most beautiful of all the

gods," said the maiden who was Loki smoothly. "When her veil comes off, I promise you will be struck down by her beauty. Now, where is her groom? Where is the wedding feast? She is so eager for this, I have barely been able to restrain her."

The sun was setting as they were led into the great hall for the wedding feast.

"What if he wants me to sit next to him?" whispered Thor to Loki.

"You have to sit next to him. That's where the bride sits."

"But he might try and put his hand on my leg," Thor whispered urgently.

"I'll sit between you," said Loki. "I'll tell him it's our custom."

Thrym sat at the head of the table, and Loki sat next to him, with Thor at the next seat on the bench.

Thrym clapped his hands and giant serving men came in. They carried five whole roast oxen, enough to feed the giants; they brought in twenty whole baked salmon, each fish the size of a ten-year-old boy; also they carried in dozens of trays of little pastries and fancies intended for the women.

They were followed by five more serving men, each one carrying a whole cask of mead, a barrel huge enough that each giant struggled beneath the weight of it.

"This meal is for the beautiful Freya!" said Thrym, and he might have said something else, but Thor had already started to eat and to drink, and it would have been rude for Thrym to have talked while the bride-to-be was eating.

A tray of pastries for the womenfolk was placed in front of Loki and Thor. Loki carefully picked out the smallest pastry. Thor just as carefully swept the rest of the pastries up, and they vanished, to the sound of munching, under the veil. The other women, who had been looking at the pastries hungrily, glared, disappointed, at the beautiful Freya.

But the beautiful Freya had not even begun to eat.

Thor ate a whole ox, all by himself. He ate seven entire salmon, leaving nothing but the bones. Each time a tray of pastries was brought to him, he devoured all the fancies and pastries on it, leaving all the other women hungry. Sometimes Loki would kick him under the table, but Thor ignored every kick and just kept eating.

Thrym tapped Loki on the shoulder. "Excuse me," he said. "But the lovely Freya has just polished off her third cask of mead."

"I'm sure she has," said the maiden who was Loki.

"Amazing. I've never seen any woman eat so ravenously. Never seen any woman eat so much, or drink so much mead."

"There is," said Loki, "an obvious explanation." He took a deep breath and watched Thor inhale another whole salmon and pull a salmon skeleton out from under his veil. It was like watching a magic trick. He wondered what the obvious explanation was.

"That makes eight salmon she's eaten," said Thrym.

"Eight days and eight nights!" said Loki suddenly. "She hasn't eaten for eight days and eight nights, she was so keen to come to the land of the giants and make love to her new husband. Now she is in your presence, she is finally eating again." The maiden turned to Thor. "It's so good to see you eating again, my dear!" she said.

Thor glared at Loki from beneath the veil.

"I should kiss her," said Thrym.

"I wouldn't advise it. Not yet," said Loki, but Thrym had already leaned over and was making kissing noises. With one huge hand he reached for Thor's veil. The maiden who was Loki put out her arm to stop him, but it was too late. Thrym had already stopped making kissing noises and had sprung back, shaken.

Thrym tapped the maiden who was Loki on the shoulder. "Can I talk with you?" he said.

"Of course."

They got up and walked across the hall.

"Why are Freya's eyes so . . . so terrifying?" asked Thrym. "It seemed as if there was a fire burning inside them. Those weren't the eyes of a beautiful woman!"

"Of course not," said the maiden who was Loki smoothly. "You wouldn't expect them to be. She hasn't slept for eight days and eight nights, mighty Thrym. She was so consumed by love for you that she dared not sleep, she was so mad to taste your love. She's burning up inside for you! That's what you're seeing in those eyes. Burning passion."

"Oh," said Thrym. "I see." He smiled, and licked his lips with a tongue bigger than a human pillow. "Well, then."

They walked back to the table. Thrym's sister had sat down in Loki's seat, beside Thor, and was tapping her fingernails on Thor's hand. "If you know what's good for you, you'll give me your rings," she was saying. "All your pretty golden rings. You'll be a stranger in this castle. You'll need someone looking out for you, otherwise things are going to get pretty nasty, so far from home. You've got so many rings. Give me some as a bridal gift. So pretty they are, all red and gold—"

"Isn't it time for the wedding?" asked Loki.

"It is!" said Thrym. He boomed at the top of his voice, "Bring in the hammer to sanctify the bride! I want to see Mjollnir placed on the beautiful Freya's lap. Let Var, the goddess of pledges between men and women, bless and consecrate our love."

It took four giants to carry Thor's hammer. They brought it in from deep inside the hall. It glinted dully in the firelight. With difficulty, they placed it on Thor's lap.

"Now," said Thrym. "Now, let me hear your beautiful voice, my love, my dove, my sweetness. Tell me that you love me. Tell me that you will be my bride. Tell me that you pledge yourself to me as women have pledged themselves to men, and men to women, since the beginning of time. What do you say?"

Thor held the haft of his hammer with a hand that was

covered with golden rings. He squeezed it reassuringly. It felt familiar and comfortable in his hand. He started laughing then, a deep, booming laugh.

"What I say," said Thor, in a voice like thunder, "is that you should not have taken my hammer."

He hit Thrym with his hammer, only once, but once was all it took. The ogre fell to the straw-covered floor, and did not rise again.

All the giants and ogres fell beneath Thor's hammer: the guests at the wedding that was never to be. Even Thrym's sister, who received a bridal gift she had not been expecting.

And when the hall was silent, Thor called "Loki?"

Loki climbed out from under the table, in his original shape, and surveyed the carnage. "Well," he said, "you appear to have dealt with the problem."

Thor was already taking off his women's skirts, with relief. He stood there wearing nothing but a shirt in a room filled with dead giants.

"There, that wasn't as bad as I had feared," he said cheerfully. "I've got my hammer back. And I had a good dinner. Let's go home."

THE MEAD
OF POETS

Do you wonder where poetry comes from? Where we get the songs we sing and the tales we tell? Do you ever ask yourself how it is that some people can dream great, wise, beautiful dreams and pass those dreams on as poetry to the world, to be sung and retold as long as the sun rises and sets, as long as the moon will wax and wane? Have you ever wondered why some people make beautiful songs and poems and tales, and some of us do not?

It is a long story, and it does no credit to anyone: there is murder in it, and trickery, lies and foolishness, seduction and pursuit. Listen.

It began not long after the dawn of time, in a war between the gods: the Aesir fought the Vanir. The Aesir were warlike gods of battle and conquest; the Vanir were softer, brother and sister gods and goddesses who made the soils fertile and the plants grow, but none the less powerful for that.

The gods of the Vanir and the Aesir were too well

matched. Neither side could win the war. And more than that, as they fought they realised that each side needed the other: that there is no joy in a brave battle unless you have fine fields and farms to feed you in the feasting that follows.

They came together to negotiate a peace, and once the negotiations were concluded, they marked their truce by each of them, Aesir and Vanir alike, one by one spitting into a vat. As their spit mingled, so was their agreement made binding.

Then they had a feast. Food was eaten, mead was drunk, and they caroused and joked and talked and boasted and laughed as the fires became glowing coals, until the sun crept up above the horizon. Then, as the Aesir and the Vanir roused themselves to leave, to wrap themselves in furs and cloth and step out into the crisp snow and the morning mist, Odin said, "It would be a shame to leave our mingled spittle behind us."

Frey and Freya, brother and sister, were leaders of the Vanir who would stay with the Aesir in Asgard from now on, under the terms of the truce. They nodded. "We could make something from it," said Frey.

"We should make a man," said Freya, and she reached into the vat.

The spittle transformed and took shape as her fingers moved, and in moments it had taken on the appearance of a man and stood naked before them.

"You are Kvasir," said Odin. "Do you know who I am?"

"You are Odin all-highest," said Kvasir. "You are Grim-nir and Third. You have other names, too many to list in this place, but I know them all, and I know the poems and the chants and the kennings that go with them."

Kvasir, made of the joining of the Aesir and the Vanir, was the wisest of the gods: he combined head and heart. The gods jostled each other to be the next to ask him questions, and his answers to them were always wise. He observed keenly, and he interpreted what he saw correctly.

Soon enough, Kvasir turned to the gods and said, "I am going to travel now. I am going to see the nine worlds, see Midgard. There are questions to be answered that I have not yet been asked."

"But you will come back to us?" they asked.

"I will come back," said Kvasir. "There is the mystery of the net, after all, which one day will need to be untangled."

"The what?" asked Thor. But Kvasir merely smiled, and he left the gods puzzling over his words, and he put on a travelling cloak, and he left Asgard and walked the rainbow bridge.

Kvasir went from town to town, from village to village. He met people of all kinds, and he treated them well and answered their questions, and there was not a place but was the better for Kvasir's stopping there.

In those days there were two dark elves who lived in a fortress by the sea. They did magic there, and feats of alchemy. Like all dwarfs, they built things, wonderful, remarkable things, in their workshop and their forge. But there were things they had not yet made, and making those things obsessed them. They were brothers, and were called Fjalar and Galar.

When they heard that Kvasir was visiting a town nearby, they set out to meet him. Fjalar and Galar found Kvasir in the great hall, answering questions for the townsfolk, amazing all who listened. He told the people how to purify water and how to make cloth from nettles. He told one woman exactly who had stolen her knife, and why. Once he was done talking and the townsfolk had fed him, the dwarfs approached.

"We have a question to ask you that you have never been asked before," they said. "But it must be asked in private. Will you come with us?"

"I will come," said Kvasir.

They walked to the fortress. The seagulls screamed, and the brooding grey clouds were the same shade as the grey of the waves. The dwarfs led Kvasir to their workshop, deep within the walls of their fortress.

"What are those?" asked Kvasir.

"They are vats. They are called Son and Bodn."

"I see. And what is that over there?"

"How can you be so wise when you do not know these things? It is a kettle. We call it Odrerir—ecstasy giver."

"And I see over here you have buckets of honey you have gathered. It is uncapped, and liquid."

"Indeed we do," said Fjalar.

Galar looked scornful. "If you were as wise as they say you are, you would know what our question to you would be before we asked it. And you would know what these things are for."

Kvasir nodded in a resigned way. "It seems to me," he said, "that if you were both intelligent and evil, you might have decided to kill your visitor and let his blood flow into the vats Son and Bodn. And then you would heat his blood gently in your kettle, Odrerir. And after that you would blend uncapped honey into the mixture and let it ferment until it became mead—the finest mead, a drink that will intoxicate anyone who drinks it but also give anyone who tastes it the gift of poetry and the gift of scholarship."

"We are intelligent," admitted Galar. "And perhaps there are those who might think us evil."

And with that he slashed Kvasir's throat, and they hung Kvasir by his feet above the vats until the last drop of his blood was drained. They warmed the blood and the honey in the kettle called Odrerir, and did other things to it of their own devising. They put berries into it, and stirred it with a stick. It bubbled, and then it ceased bubbling, and both of them sipped it and laughed, and each of the brothers found the verse and the poetry inside himself that he had never let out.

The gods came the next morning. "Kvasir," they said. "He was last seen with you."

"Yes," said the dwarfs. "He came back with us, but

when he realised that we are only dwarfs, and foolish and lacking in wisdom, he choked on his own knowledge. If only we had been able to ask him questions."

"He died, you say?"

"Yes," said Fjalar and Galar, and they gave the gods Kvasir's bloodless body to take back to Asgard, for a god's funeral and perhaps (because gods are not as others, and death is not always permanent for them) for a god's eventual return.

Thus it was that the dwarfs had the mead of wisdom and poetry, and any person who wished to taste it needed to beg it from the dwarfs. But Galar and Fjalar gave the mead only to those they liked, and they liked nobody but themselves.

Still, there were those to whom they had obligations. The giant Gilling, for example, and his wife: the dwarfs invited them to come and visit their fortress, and one winter's day they came.

"Let us go rowing in our boat," the dwarfs told Gilling.

The giant's weight made the boat ride low in the water, and the dwarfs rowed the boat on to the rocks just under the surface. Always before their boat had floated serenely above the rocks. Not this time. The boat crashed on to the rocks and overturned, throwing the giant into the sea.

"Swim back to the boat," the brothers called to Gilling.

"I cannot swim," he said, and that was the last thing he said, for a wave filled his open mouth with salt water, and his head hit the rocks, and in a moment he was lost to view.

Fjalar and Galar righted their boat and went home.

Gilling's wife was waiting for them.

"Where is my husband?" she asked.

"Him?" said Galar. "Oh, he's dead."

"Drowned," added Fjalar helpfully.

At this the giant's wife wailed and sobbed as if each cry were being ripped from her soul. She called to her dead husband and swore she would love him always, and she cried and moaned and wept.

"Hush!" said Galar. "Your weeping and wailing hurts my ears. It's very loud. I expect that's because you're a giant."

But the giant's wife simply wept the louder.

"Here," said Fjalar. "Would it help if we showed you the place where your husband died?"

She sniffed, and nodded, and cried and wailed and keened for her husband, who would never come back to her.

"Stand just over there and we will point it out to you," said Fjalar, showing her exactly where she should stand, that she should go through the great door and stand beneath the wall of the fortress. And he nodded to his brother, who scurried off up the steps to the wall above.

As Gilling's wife walked through the door, Galar dropped a huge stone on her head, and she fell, her skull half crushed.

"Good job," said Fjalar. "I was getting very tired of those dreadful noises."

They pushed the woman's lifeless body off the rocks and into the sea. The fingers of the grey waves dragged her body away from them, and Gilling's wife and Gilling were reunited in death.

The dwarfs shrugged, and believed themselves to be extremely clever in their fortress by the sea.

They drank the mead of poetry each night, and declaimed great and beautiful verses to each other, made mighty sagas about the death of Gilling and Gilling's wife, which they declaimed from the rooftop of their fortress, and eventually each night they slept, insensible, and woke where they had sat down or fallen the night before.

One day they woke as usual, but they did not wake in their fortress.

They woke on the floor of their boat, and a giant whom they did not recognise was rowing it into the waves. The sky was dark with storm clouds and the sea was black. The waves were high and rough, and the salt water splashed over the side of the dwarfs' boat, soaking them.

"Who are you?" asked the dwarfs.

"I am Suttung," said the giant. "I heard you were bragging to the wind and the waves and the world about having killed my father and mother."

"Ah," said Galar. "Does that explain why you have tied us up?"

"It does," said Suttung.

"Perhaps you are taking us to a glorious place," said Fjalar hopefully, "where you will untie us, and there we will feast and drink and laugh and become the best of friends."

"I do not believe so," said Suttung.

It was low tide. There were rocks jutting out above the water. They were the same rocks upon which at high tide the dwarfs' boat had overturned, on which Gilling had drowned. Suttung picked up each of the dwarfs, took him from the bottom of the boat and placed him on the rocks.

"These rocks will be covered by the sea at high tide," said Fjalar. "Our hands are tied behind our backs. We cannot swim. If you leave us here, we will undoubtedly drown."

"That is certainly the intention," said Suttung. He smiled then, for the first time. "And as you drown I shall sit in this, your boat, and I shall watch the sea take you both. Then I shall return home to Jotunheim, and I will tell my brother, Baugi, and my daughter, Gunnlod, how you died, and we will be satisfied that my mother and my father were appropriately avenged."

The sea began to rise. It covered the dwarfs' feet, and then it came up to their navels. Soon enough the dwarfs' beards were floating in the foam and there was panic in their eyes.

"Mercy!" they called.

"Like the mercy you gave my mother and my father?"

"We will compensate you for their deaths! We will make it up to you! We will pay you."

"I do not believe that you dwarfs possess anything

that could compensate me for my parents' deaths. I am a wealthy giant. I have many servants in my mountain fastness, and all the riches I could dream of. Gold I have, and precious stones, and iron enough to make a thousand swords. I am the master of mighty magics. What could you give me that I do not already have?" asked Suttung.

The dwarfs said nothing at all.

The waves continued to rise.

"We have mead, the mead of poetry," sputtered Galar as the water brushed his lips.

"Made of Kvasir's blood, wisest of all the gods!" shouted Fjalar. "Two vats and a kettle, all filled with it! No one has it but us, no one in the whole world!"

Suttung scratched his head. "I must think about this. I must ponder. I must reflect."

"Do not stop and think! If you think, we will drown!" shouted Fjalar over the roar of the waves.

The tide rose. Waves were splashing over the dwarfs' heads, and they were gulping air, and their eyes were round with fear when Suttung the giant reached out and plucked first Fjalar and then Galar from the waves.

"The mead of poetry will be adequate compensation. It is a fair price, if you throw in a few other things, and I am sure you dwarfs have a few other things. I shall spare your lives."

He tossed them, still bound and soaking, into the bottom of the boat, where they wriggled uncomfortably, like a couple of bearded lobsters, and he rowed back to shore.

Suttung took the mead the dwarfs had made from Kvasir's blood. He took other things from them as well, and he left that place and he left those dwarfs, who were, all things considered, happy enough to have got away with their lives.

Fjalar and Galar told people who passed their fortress the story of how ill-used they had been by Suttung. They told it in the market when next they went to trade. They told it when ravens were near.

In Asgard, at his high seat, Odin sat, and his ravens, Huginn and Muninn, whispered to him of the things they had seen and heard as they had wandered the world. Odin's one eye flashed when he heard the tale of Suttung's mead.

The people who heard the story called the mead of poetry "the ship of the dwarfs" since it had floated Fjalar and Galar off the rocks and taken them safely home; they called it Suttung's mead; they called it the liquid of Odrerir or Bodn or Son.

Odin listened to his ravens' words. He called for his cloak and his hat. He sent for the gods and told them to prepare three enormous wooden vats, the largest vats that they could build, and to have them waiting by the gates of Asgard. He told the gods he would be leaving them to walk the world, and might be some time.

"I will take two things with me," said Odin. "I need a whetstone, to sharpen a blade with. The finest we have here. And I wish to have the auger, the drill, called Rati."

Rati means "drill", and Rati was the finest drill the gods possessed. It could drill deeply, and drill through the hardest rock.

Odin tossed the whetstone into the air and caught it again and put it into his pouch beside the auger. Then he walked away.

"I wonder what he's going to do," said Thor.

"Kvasir would have known," said Frigg. "He knew everything."

"Kvasir is dead," said Loki. "As for me, I do not care where the all-father is going, or why."

"I am off to help build the wooden vats that the all-father requested," said Thor.

Suttung had given the precious mead to his daughter, Gunnlod, to watch over inside the mountain called Hnit-bjorg, in the heart of giant country. Odin did not go to the mountain. Instead he went directly to the farmland owned by Suttung's brother, Baugi.

It was spring, and the fields were high with grasses to be cut for hay. Baugi had nine slaves, giants like himself, and they were cutting the grass for hay with huge scythes, each scythe the size of a small tree.

Odin watched them. When they stopped work, when the sun was at its highest, to eat their provisions, Odin sauntered over to them and said, "I have been watching you all work. Tell me, why does your master let you cut grass with such blunt scythes?"

"Our blades are not blunt," said one of the workers.

"Why would you say that?" asked another. "Our blades are the sharpest."

"Let me show you what a well-sharpened blade can do," said Odin. He took the whetstone from his pouch and drew it along first one scythe blade, then another, until each blade glimmered in the sun. The giants stood around him awkwardly, watching him as he worked. "Now," said Odin, "try them out."

The giant slaves swept their scythes through the meadow grass and gasped and exclaimed with pleasure. The blades were so sharp they made cutting the grass effortless. The blades swept through the thickest stalks and met with no resistance.

"This is wonderful!" they told Odin. "Can we buy your whetstone?"

"Buy it?" said the all-father. "Absolutely not. Let us do something more fair and more fun. All of you, come here. Stand in a group, each man holding his scythe tightly. Stand closer."

"We can stand no closer," said one of the giant slaves. "For the scythes are very sharp."

"You are wise," said Odin. He held up the whetstone. "I tell you this. The one of you who catches it, he alone shall have it!" and so saying, he tossed the whetstone into the air.

Nine giants jumped at the whetstone as it descended, each reaching with his free hand, paying no attention to the scythe he held (each scythe with a blade sharpened by the all-father at his whetstone, whetted to a perfect sharpness).

They jumped and they reached and the blades glinted in the sun.

There was a spray and a spurt of crimson in the sunlight, and the bodies of the slaves crumpled and twitched and one by one fell to the freshly cut grass. Odin stepped over the bodies of the giants, retrieved the whetstone of the gods, and placed it back in his pouch.

Each of the nine slaves had died with his throat cut by his fellow's blade.

Odin walked to the hall of Baugi, Suttung's brother, and asked for lodging for the night. "I am called Bolverkr," said Odin.

"Bolverkr," said Baugi. "A dismal name. It means 'worker of terrible things'."

"Only to my enemies," said the person who called himself Bolverkr. "My friends appreciate the things I do. I can do the work of nine men, and I will work tirelessly and without complaint."

"Lodging for the night is yours," said Baugi, sighing. "But you have come to me on a dark day. Yesterday I was a rich man, with many fields and with nine slaves to plant and to harvest, to labour and to build. Tonight I still own my fields and my animals, but all my servants are dead. They slew each other. I do not know why."

"A dark day indeed," said Bolverkr, who was Odin. "Can you not get other workmen?"

"Not this year," sighed Baugi. "It is already spring. The good workers are already working for my brother Suttung, and few enough people come here in the way of things. You are the first traveller who has asked me for lodging and hospitality in many a year."

"And lucky you are that I did. For I can do the work of nine men."

"You are not a giant," said Baugi. "You are a little shrimp of a thing. How could you do the work of one of my servants, let alone nine of them?"

"If I cannot do the work of your nine men," said Bolverkr, "then you need not pay me. But if I do . . ."

"Yes?"

"Even in distant parts we have heard tales about your brother Suttung's extraordinary mead. They say it bestows the gift of poetry on anyone who drinks it."

"This is true. Suttung was never a poet when we were young. I was the poet in the family. But since he has returned with the dwarfs' mead, he has become a poet and a dreamer."

"If I work for you, and plant and build and harvest for you, and do the work of your dead servants, I would like to taste your brother Suttung's mead."

"But . . ." Baugi's forehead creased. "But that is not mine to give. It is Suttung's."

"A pity," said Bolverkr. "Then I wish you luck in getting the harvest in this year."

"Wait! It is not mine, true. But if you can do what you

say, I will go with you to see my brother Suttung. And I will do all I can to help you taste his mead."

"Then," said Bolverkr, "we have a deal."

Never was there a harder worker than Bolverkr. He worked the land harder than twenty men, let alone nine. Single-handed he looked after the animals. Single-handed he harvested the crops. He worked the land, and the land repaid him a thousandfold.

"Bolverkr," said Baugi as the first mists of winter rolled down the mountain, "you are misnamed. For you have worked nothing but good."

"Have I done the work of nine men?"

"You have, and nine again."

"Then will you help me to get a taste of Suttung's mead?"

"I shall!"

The next morning they rose early and walked and walked and walked, and by evening they had left Baugi's land and reached Suttung's, on the edge of the mountains. By nightfall they reached Suttung's huge hall.

"Greetings, brother Suttung," said Baugi. "This is Bolverkr, my servant for the summer, and my friend." And he told Suttung of his agreement with Bolverkr. "So you see," he concluded, "I must ask you to give him a taste of the mead of poetry."

Suttung's eyes were like chips of ice. "No," he said flatly.

"No?" said Baugi.

"No, I will not give away a single drop of that mead. Not one drop. I have it safe in its vats, in Bodn and Son and the kettle Odrerir. Those vats are deep inside the mountain of Hnitbjorg, which opens only to my command. My daughter, Gunnlod, guards it. This servant of yours cannot taste it. You cannot taste it."

"But," said Baugi, "it was blood compensation for our parents' deaths. Don't I deserve the smallest measure of it, to show Bolverkr here that I am an honourable giant?"

"No," said Suttung. "You don't."

They left his hall.

Baugi was disconsolate. He walked with his shoulders hunched high and his mouth drooping down. Every few paces, Baugi would apologise to Bolverkr. "I did not think my brother would be so unreasonable," he would say.

"He is indeed unreasonable," said Bolverkr, who was Odin in disguise. "But you and I could play a little trick or two on him, so that he would not be so high and mighty in future. So that next time he will listen to his brother."

"We could do that," said the giant Baugi, and he stood straighter, and the corners of his mouth tightened into something that almost resembled a smile. "What are we going to do?"

"First," said Bolverkr, "we will climb Hnitbjorg, the beating mountain."

They climbed Hnitbjorg together, the giant going first, and Bolverkr, doll-sized in comparison, never falling behind. They clambered up the paths that the mountain sheep and goats made, and then they scrambled up rocks until they were high in the mountain. The first snows of winter had fallen on the ice that had not melted from the winter before. They heard the wind as it whistled about the mountain. They heard the cries of birds far below them. And there was something else they could hear.

It was a noise like a human voice. It seemed to be coming from the rocks of the mountain, but it was always distant, as if it were coming from inside the mountain itself.

"What noise is that?" asked Bolverkr.

Baugi frowned. "It sounds like my niece Gunnlod, singing."

"Then we will stop here."

From his leather pouch Bolverkr produced the auger called Rati. "Here," he said. "You are a giant, and big and strong. Why don't you use this auger to drill into the side of the mountain?"

Baugi took the auger. He pushed it against the mountainside and began to twist. The tip of the auger drilled into the mountainside like a screw into soft cork. Baugi turned it and turned it, again and again.

"Done it," said Baugi. He pulled out the auger.

Bolverkr leaned over the hole made by the drill and blew into it. Chips and the dust of rocks blew back at him. "I have just learned two things," said Bolverkr.

"What two things are these?" asked Baugi.

"That we are not yet through the mountain," said Bolverkr. "You must keep drilling."

"That is only one thing," said Baugi. But Bolverkr said nothing more on that high mountainside, where the icy winds clawed and clutched at them. Baugi pushed the drill Rati back into its hole and began to turn it once more.

It was getting dark when Baugi pulled the auger from the hole again. "It broke through into the inside of the mountain," he said.

Bolverkr said nothing, but he blew gently into the hole, and this time he saw the chips of rock blow inward.

As he blew, he was aware that something was coming towards him from behind. Bolverkr transformed himself then: he turned himself into a snake, and the sharp auger plunged into the place where his head had been.

"The second thing I learned when you lied to me," hissed the snake to Baugi, who stood, astonished, holding the auger like a weapon, "was that you would betray me." And with a flick of its tail, the snake vanished into the hole in the mountainside.

Baugi struck again with the auger, but the snake was gone, and he flung the drill from him angrily and heard it clatter on the rocks below. He thought about going back to Suttung's hall and once he was there telling his brother that he had helped bring a powerful magician up Hnitbjorg, had even helped him to get inside the mountain. He imagined Suttung's reaction to this news.

And then, his shoulders slumping and his mouth drooping, Baugi climbed down the mountain and trudged off home, to his own hearth and his own hall. Whatever happened in the future to his brother or to his brother's precious mead, why, it was nothing to do with *him*.

Bolverkr slid in snake shape through the hole in the mountain until the hole ended and he found himself in a huge cavern.

The cavern was lit by crystals, with a cold light. Odin transformed himself from snake shape into man shape once more, and not just a man but a huge man, giant-sized, and well formed. Then he walked forward, following the sound of song.

Gunnlod, the daughter of Suttung, stood in the cavern in front of a locked door, behind which were the vats called Son and Bodn and the kettle Odrerir. She held a sharp sword in her hands, and she sang to herself as she stood.

"Well met, brave maiden!" said Odin.

Gunnlod stared at him. "I do not know who you are," she said. "Name yourself, stranger, and tell me why I should let you live. I am Gunnlod, guardian of this place."

"I am Bolverkr," said Odin, "and I deserve death, I know, for daring to come to this place. But stay your hand, and let me look upon you."

Gunnlod said, "My father, Suttung, set me on guard here, to protect the mead of poetry."

Bolverkr shrugged. "Why would I care for the mead of poetry? I came here only because I had heard of the beauty and the courage and the virtue of Gunnlod, Suttung's daughter. I told myself, 'If she just lets you look at her, it will be worth it. If, of course, she is as beautiful as they say in the tales.' That was what I thought."

Gunnlod stared at the handsome giant in front of her. "And was it worth it, Bolverkr-who-is-about-to-die?"

"More than worth it," he told her. "For you are more beautiful than any tale I have ever heard or any song that any bard could compose. More beautiful than a mountain peak, more beautiful than a glacier, more beautiful than a field of fresh-fallen snow at dawn."

Gunnlod looked down, and her cheeks reddened.

"Can I sit beside you?" asked Bolverkr.

Gunnlod nodded, saying nothing.

She had food there in the mountain, and drink, and they ate and they drank.

After they ate, they kissed gently in the darkness.

After their lovemaking, Bolverkr said sadly, "I wish I could taste one sip of the mead from the vat called Son. Then I could make a true song about your eyes, and all men would sing it when they wanted to sing of beauty."

"One sip?" she asked.

"A sip so small nobody would ever know," he said. "But I am in no hurry. You are more important than that. Let me show you how important to me you are."

And he pulled her to him.

They made love in the darkness. When they had finished and were curled up together, naked skin touching skin, whispering endearments, then Bolverkr sighed mournfully.

"What is wrong?" asked Gunnlod.

"I wish I had the skill to sing of your lips, how soft they are, how much better they are than the lips of any other girl. I think that would be an excellent song."

"That is indeed unfortunate," agreed Gunnlod. "For my lips are very attractive. I often think they are my best feature."

"Perhaps, but you have so many perfect features, picking the best is so difficult. But if I were to take the tiniest taste from the vat called Bodn, the poetry would enter my soul and I would be able to make a poem about your lips that would last until the sun is eaten by a wolf."

"Only the *tiniest* sip, though," she said. "Because Father would get quite irritable if he thought I was giving away his mead to every good-looking stranger who penetrated this mountain fastness."

They walked the caverns, holding hands and occasionally brushing lips. Gunnlod showed Bolverkr the doors and the windows that she could open from inside the mountain, through which Suttung sent her food and drink, and Bolverkr appeared to pay no attention; he explained that he was not interested in anything that was not about Gunnlod, or her eyes or her lips or her fingers or her hair. Gunnlod laughed and told him that he did not mean any of his fine words and he obviously could not want to make love with her again.

He hushed her lips with his lips, and once again they made love.

When they were both perfectly satisfied, Bolverkr began to weep in the darkness.

"What's wrong, my love?" asked Gunnlod.

"Kill me," sobbed Bolverkr. "Kill me now! For I will never be able to make a poem about the perfection of your hair and your skin, of the sound of your voice, of the feel of your fingers. The beauty of Gunnlod is impossible to describe."

"Well," she said, "I suppose it can't be easy to make such a poem. But I doubt it's impossible."

"Perhaps . . ."

"Yes?"

"Perhaps the smallest sip from the kettle Odrerir would give me the lyrical skills to conjure your beauty for generations still to come," he suggested, his sobs ceasing.

"Yes, perhaps it would. But it would have to be the *smallest* of smallest sips . . ."

"Show me the kettle, and I will show you just how small a sip I can take."

Gunnlod unlocked the door, and in moments she and Bolverkr were standing in front of the kettle and the two vats. The smell of the mead of poetry was heady on the air.

"Just the tiniest of sips," she told him. "For three poems about me that will echo down through the ages."

"Of course, my darling." Bolverkr grinned in the darkness. If she had been looking at him then, she would have known something was wrong.

With his first drink he drank every drop of the kettle Odrerir.

With his second, he drained the vat called Bodn.

With his third, he emptied the vat called Son.

Gunnlod was no fool. She realised that she had been betrayed, and she attacked him. She was strong and fast, but Odin did not stay to fight. He ran from there. He pulled the door closed and locked her inside.

In the blink of an eye he became a huge eagle. Odin screeched as he flapped his wings, and the mountain doors opened, and he rose into the skies.

Gunnlod's screams pierced the dawn.

In his hall, Suttung woke and ran outside. He looked up and saw the eagle and knew what must have happened. Suttung too transformed himself into eagle shape.

The two eagles flew so high that from the ground they were the tiniest of pinpricks in the sky. They flew so fast that their flight sounded like the roar of a hurricane.

In Asgard, Thor said, "It is time."

He hauled the three huge wooden vats into the courtyard.

The gods of Asgard watched the eagles screaming through the sky towards them. It was a close thing. Suttung was fast, and close behind Odin, his beak almost touching Odin's tail feathers as they reached Asgard.

When Odin approached the hall, he began to spit: a fountain of mead spurted from his beak into the vats, one after another, like a father bird bringing food for his children.

Ever since then, we know that those people who can make magic with their words, who can make poems and sagas and weave tales, have tasted the mead of poetry. When we hear a fine poet, we say that they have tasted Odin's gift.

There. That is the story of the mead of poetry and how it was given to the world. It is a story filled with dishonour and deceit, with murder and trickery. But it is not quite the whole story. There is one more thing to tell you. The delicate among you should stop your ears, or read no further.

Here is the last thing, and a shameful admission it is. When the all-father in eagle form had almost reached the vats, with Suttung immediately behind him, Odin blew some of the mead out of his behind, a splattery wet fart of foul-smelling mead right in Suttung's face, blinding the giant and throwing him off Odin's trail.

No one, then or now, wanted to drink the mead that came out of Odin's arse. But whenever you hear bad poets declaiming their bad poetry, filled with foolish similes and ugly rhymes, you will know which of the meads they have tasted.

THOR'S JOURNEY
TO THE LAND
OF THE GIANTS

I

Thialfi and his sister, Roskva, lived with their father, Egil, and their mother on a farm at the edge of wild country. Beyond their farm were monsters and giants and wolves, and many times Thialfi walked into trouble and had to outrun it. He could run faster than anyone or anything. Living at the edge of the wild country meant that Thialfi and Roskva were used to miracles and strange things happening in their world.

Nothing as strange, however, as the day that two visitors from Asgard, Loki and Thor, arrived at their farm in a chariot pulled by two huge goats, whom Thor called Snarler and Grinder. The gods expected lodging for the night, and food. The gods were huge and powerful.

"We have no food for the likes of you," said Roskva apologetically. "We have vegetables, but it's been a hard winter, and we don't even have any chickens left."

Thor grunted. Then he took his knife and killed both his goats. He skinned their corpses. He put the goats in the huge stewpot that hung above the fire, while Roskva and her mother cut up their winter stores of vegetables and dropped them into the stewpot.

Loki took Thialfi aside. The boy was intimidated by Loki: his green eyes, his scarred lips, his smile. Loki said, "You know, the marrow of the bones of those goats is the finest thing a young man can eat. Such a shame that Thor always keeps it all for himself. If you want to grow up to be as strong as Thor, you should eat the goat bone marrow."

When the food was ready, Thor took a whole goat as his portion, leaving the meat of the other goat for the other five people.

He put the goatskins down on the ground, and as he ate, he threw the bones on to his goatskin. "Put your bones on the other goatskin," he told them. "And don't break or chew any of the bones. Just eat the meat."

You think you can eat fast? You should have seen Loki devour his food. One moment it was in front of him, and the next it was gone and he was wiping his lips with the back of his hand.

The rest of them ate more slowly. But Thialfi could not forget what Loki had said to him, and when Thor left the table for a call of nature, Thialfi took his knife and split one of the goat's leg bones and ate some of the marrow from it. He put the broken bone down on the goatskin and covered it with undamaged bones, so nobody would know.

They all slept in the great hall that night.

In the morning, Thor covered the bones with the goat-skins. He took his hammer, Mjollnir, and held it up high. He said, "Snarler, be whole." A flash of lightning: Snarler stretched itself, bleated, and began to graze. Thor said, "Grinder, be whole," and Grinder did the same. And then it staggered and limped awkwardly over to Snarler, and it let out a high-pitched bleat as if it were in pain.

"Grinder's hind leg is broken," said Thor. "Bring me wood and cloth."

He made a splint for his goat's leg, and he bandaged it up. And when that was done, he looked at the family, and Thialfi did not think he had ever seen anything quite as scary as Thor's burning red eyes. Thor's fist was wrapped around the shaft of his hammer. "Somebody here broke that bone," he told them, in a voice like thunder. "I gave you people food, I asked only one thing of you, and yet you betrayed me."

"I did it," said Thialfi. "I broke the bone."

Loki was trying to look serious, but even so, he was smiling at the corners of his mouth. It was not a reassuring smile.

Thor hefted his hammer. "I ought to destroy this entire farm," he muttered, and Egil looked scared, and Egil's wife began to weep. Then Thor said, "Tell me why I should not turn this whole place to rubble."

Egil said nothing. Thialfi stood up. He said, "It has nothing to do with my father. He didn't know what I had done. Punish me, not him. Look at me: I'm a really fast runner. I can learn. Let my parents be, and I'll be your bondservant."

His sister, Roskva, stood up. "He is not leaving without me," she said. "Take him, you take both of us."

Thor pondered this for a moment. Then: "Very well. For now, Roskva, you will stay here and tend Snarler and Grinder while Grinder's leg heals. When I return, I will collect all three of you." He turned to Thialfi. "And you can come with me and Loki. We are going to Utgard."

II

The world beyond the farm was wilderness, and Thor and Loki and Thialfi travelled east, towards Jotunheim, home of the giants, and towards the sea.

It became colder the farther east they went. Freezing winds blew, draining them of any warmth. Shortly before sunset, when there was still enough light to see, they looked for a place to shelter for the night. Thor and Thialfi found nothing. Loki was away the longest. He came back with a puzzled look on his face. "There's an odd sort of house over that way," he said.

"How odd?" asked Thor.

"It's just one huge room. No windows, and the doorway is enormous but it has no door. It's like a huge cave."

The cold wind numbed their fingers and stung their cheeks. Thor said, "We shall check it out."

The main hall went back a long way. "There could be

beasts or monsters back there," said Thor. "Let's set up by the entrance."

They did just that. It was as Loki had described—a huge building, one huge hall, with a long room off to one side. They made a fire by the entrance and slept there for an hour or so, until they were woken by a noise.

"What's that?" said Thialfi.

"An earthquake?" said Thor. The ground was trembling. Something roared. It might have been a volcano, or an avalanche of great rocks, or a hundred furious bears.

"I don't think so," said Loki. "Let's move into the side room. Just to be safe."

Loki and Thialfi slept in the side room, and the tumbling-roaring noise continued until daybreak. Thor stationed himself at the door to the house all night, holding his hammer. He had been getting more irritable as the night wore on, and wanted only to explore and to attack whatever was rumbling and shaking the earth. As soon as the sky began to lighten, Thor walked into the forest without waking his companions, looking for the source of the sound.

There were, he realised as he got closer, different sounds, which occurred in sequence. First a rumbling roar, followed by a humming, and then a softer sort of whistling noise, piercing enough to make Thor's head ache and his teeth hurt each time he heard it.

Thor reached the top of a hill and looked at the world beneath him.

Stretched out in the valley below was the biggest

person Thor had ever seen. His hair and beard were blacker than charcoal; his skin was as white as a snow field. The giant's eyes were closed, and he was regularly snoring: that was the rumble-hum and whistle that Thor had been listening to. Every time the giant snored the ground shook. That was the shaking they had felt in the night. The giant was so big that by comparison Thor might have been a beetle or an ant.

Thor reached down to his belt of strength, Megingjord, and pulled it tight, doubling his strength to make sure that he was strong enough to battle even the hugest of giants.

As Thor watched, the giant opened his eyes: they were a piercing icy blue. The giant did not seem immediately threatening, though.

"Hello," called Thor.

"Good morning!" called the black-haired giant, in a voice like an avalanche. "They call me Skrymir. It means 'big fellow'. They are sarcastic, my lot, calling a runty little chap like me Big Fellow, but there you are. Now, where's my glove? I had two, you know, last night, but I dropped one." He held up his hands: his right hand had a huge mittenlike leather glove on it. The other was bare. "Oh! There it is."

He reached down to the far side of the hill Thor had climbed, and he picked up something that was obviously another mitten. "Odd. Something's in it," he said, and gave it a shake. Thor recognised their home of the previous night just as Thialfi and Loki came tumbling out of the mouth of the glove and landed in the snow beneath.

Skrymir put his left mitten on and looked happily at his mittened hands. "We can travel together," he said. "If you're willing."

Thor looked at Loki and Loki looked at Thor and both of them looked at young Thialfi, who shrugged. "I can keep up," he said, confident of his speed.

"Very well," shouted Thor.

They ate breakfast with the giant: he pulled whole cows and sheep from his provision bag and crunched them down; the three companions ate more sparingly. After the meal, Skrymir said, "Here. I'll carry your provisions inside my bag. Less for you to carry, and we will all eat together when we camp tonight." He put their food in his bag, did up the laces, and strode off towards the east.

Thor and Loki ran after the giant with the untiring pace of gods. Thialfi ran as fast as any man has ever run, but even he found it hard to keep up as the hours went by, and sometimes it seemed that the giant was just another mountain in the distance, his head lost in the clouds.

They caught up with Skrymir as evening fell. He had found a camp for them beneath a huge old oak tree and had made himself comfortable nearby, his head resting on a great boulder. "I'm not hungry," he told them. "Don't you worry about me. I'm going to get an early night. Your provisions are in my bag, up against the tree. Goodnight."

He began to snore. As the familiar rumble-hum and

whistle shook the trees, Thialfi climbed the giant's provision bag. He called down to Thor and Loki, "I cannot undo the laces. They are too tough for me. They might as well be made out of iron."

"I can bend iron," said Thor, and he leapt to the top of the provision bag and began to tug on the laces.

"Well?" asked Loki.

Thor grunted and hauled, hauled and grunted. Then he shrugged. "I don't think we'll be having dinner tonight," he said. "Not unless this damnable giant undoes the laces on his bag for us."

He looked at the giant. He looked at Mjollnir, his hammer. Then he clambered down the bag, and he made his way on to the top of Skrymir's sleeping head. He raised the hammer and slammed it down on Skrymir's forehead.

Skrymir opened one eye sleepily. "I think a leaf just fell on my head and woke me up," he said. "Have you all finished eating? Are you ready for bed? Don't blame you if you are. Long day." And he rolled over, closed his eyes, and began to snore once again.

Loki and Thialfi managed to fall asleep despite the noise, but Thor could not sleep. He was angry, he was hungry, and he did not trust this giant, out in the eastern wilderness. At midnight he was still hungry, and he had had enough of the snoring. He clambered up on to the giant's head once more. He positioned himself between the giant's eyebrows.

Thor spat into his hands. He adjusted his belt of

strength. He raised Mjollnir over his head. And with all his might, he swung. He was certain that the hammer head sank into Skrymir's forehead.

It was too dark to see the colour of the giant's eyes, but they opened. "Whoa," the big fellow said. "Thor? Are you there? I think an acorn just fell off the tree on to my head. What time is it?"

"It's midnight," said Thor.

"Well, then, see you in the morning." Giant snores shook the ground and made the tops of the trees tremble.

It was dawn but not yet day when Thor, hungrier, angrier and still sleepless, resolved to strike one final blow that would silence the snoring forever. This time he aimed for the giant's temple, and he hit Skrymir with all his strength. Never was there such a blow. Thor heard it echo from the mountaintops.

"You know," said Skrymir, "I think a bit of bird's nest just dropped on my head. Twigs. I don't know." He yawned and stretched. Then he got to his feet. "Well, I'm done sleeping. Time to be on our way. Are you three headed to Utgard? They will look after you well there. I guarantee you a mighty feast, horns of ale, and afterwards wrestling and racing and contests of strength. They like their fun in Utgard. That's due east—just head that way, where the sky is lightening. Me, I'll be off to the north." He gave them a gap-toothed grin, which would have seemed foolish and vacant if his eyes had not been so very blue and so very sharp.

Then he leaned over and put a hand beside his mouth, as if he did not wish to be overheard, an effect slightly lessened by his whisper, which was loud enough to deafen. "I couldn't help overhearing you fellows back then, when you were saying how very big I was. And I suppose you thought you were complimenting me. But if ever you make it to the north, you'll meet *proper* giants, the really big fellows. And you'll find out what a shrimp I really am."

Skrymir grinned again, and then he stomped off towards the north, and the ground rumbled beneath his feet.

III

They travelled east through Jotunheim, always travelling towards the sunrise, for some days.

At first they thought they were looking at a normal-sized fortress and that it was relatively close to them; they walked towards it, hurrying their pace, but it did not grow or change or seem closer. As the days passed they realised how big it was and just how far away.

"Is that Utgard?" asked Thialfi.

Loki seemed almost serious as he said, "It is. This is where my family came from."

"Have you ever been here before?"

"I have not."

They strode up to the fortress gate, seeing no one. They could hear what sounded like a party going on inside. The gate was higher than most cathedrals. It had metal bars covering it, of a size that would have kept any unwanted giants at a respectable distance.

Thor shouted, but no one responded to his calls.

"Shall we go in?" he asked Loki and Thialfi.

They ducked and climbed under the bars of the gate. The travellers walked through the courtyard and into the great hall. There were benches as high as treetops, with giants sitting on them. Thor strode in. Thialfi was terrified, but he walked beside Thor, and Loki walked behind them.

They could see the king of the giants, sitting on the highest chair, at the end of the hall. They crossed the hall, and then they bowed deeply.

The king had a narrow, intelligent face and flame-red hair. His eyes were an icy blue. He looked at the travellers, and he raised an eyebrow.

"Good lord," he said. "It's an invasion of tiny toddlers. No, my mistake. *You* must be the famous Thor of the Aesir, which means *you* must be Loki, Laufey's son. I knew your mother a little. Hello, small relation. I am Utgardaloki, the Loki of Utgard. And you are?"

"Thialfi," said Thialfi. "I am Thor's bondservant."

"Welcome, all of you, to Utgard," said Utgardaloki. "The finest place in the world, for those who are remarkable. Anyone here who is, in craft or cunning, beyond everyone else in the world is welcome. Can any of you do anything special? What about you, little relative? What can you do that's unique?"

"I can eat faster than anybody," said Loki, without boasting.

"How interesting. I have my servant here. His name is, amusingly enough, Logi. Would you like an eating competition with him?"

Loki shrugged, as if it were all the same to him.

Utgardaloki clapped his hands, and a long wooden trough was brought in, with all manner of roasted animals in it: geese and oxen and sheep, goats and rabbits and deer. When he clapped his hands again, Loki began to eat, starting at the far end of the trough and working his way inward.

He ate hard, he ate single-mindedly, he ate as if he had only one goal in life: to eat all he could as fast as he could. His hands and mouth were a blur.

Logi and Loki met at the middle of the table.

Utgardaloki looked down from his throne. "Well," he said, "you both ate at the same speed—not bad!—but Logi ate the bones of the animals, and yes, it appears he also ate the wooden trough it was served in. Loki ate all the flesh, it's true, but he barely touched the bones and he didn't even make a start on the trough. So this round goes to Logi."

Utgardaloki looked at Thialfi. "You," he said. "Boy. What can you do?"

Thialfi shrugged. He was the fastest person he knew. He could outrun startled rabbits, outrun a bird in flight. He said, "I can run."

"Then," said Utgardaloki, "you shall run."

They walked outside, and there, on a level piece of ground, was a track, perfect for running. A number of giants stood and waited by the track, rubbing their hands together and blowing on them for warmth.

"You're just a boy, Thialfi," said Utgardaloki. "So I will not have you run against a grown man. Where is our little Hugi?"

A giant-child stepped forward, so thin he might not have been there, not much bigger than Loki or Thor. The child looked at Utgardaloki and said nothing, but he smiled. Thialfi was not certain that the boy had been there before he had been called. But he was there now.

Hugi and Thialfi stood side by side at the starting line, and they waited.

"Go!" called Utgardaloki, in a voice like thunder, and the boys began to run. Thialfi ran as he had never run before, but he watched Hugi pull ahead and reach the finish line when he was barely halfway there.

Utgardaloki called, "Victory goes to Hugi." Then he crouched down beside Thialfi. "You will need to run faster if you have a hope of beating Hugi," said the giant. "Still, I've not seen any human run like that before. Run faster, Thialfi."

Thialfi stood beside Hugi at the starting line once more. Thialfi was panting, and his heart was pounding in his ears. He knew how fast he had run, and yet Hugi had run faster, and Hugi seemed completely at ease. He was not even breathing hard. The giant-child looked at Thialfi and smiled again. There was something about Hugi that reminded Thialfi of Utgardaloki, and he wondered if the giant-child was Utgardaloki's son.

"Go!"

They ran. Thialfi ran as he had never run before, moving so fast that the world seemed to contain only himself and Hugi. And Hugi was still ahead of him the whole way. Hugi reached the finish line when Thialfi was still five, perhaps ten seconds away.

Thialfi knew that he had been close to winning that time, knew that all he had to do was give it all he had.

"Let us run again," he panted.

"Very well," said Utgardaloki. "You can run again. You are fast, young man, but I do not believe you can win. Still, we will let the final race decide the outcome."

Hugi stepped over to the starting line. Thialfi stood next to him. He could not even hear Hugi breathing.

"Good luck," said Thialfi.

"This time," said Hugi, in a voice that seemed to sound in Thialfi's head, "you will see me run."

"Go!" called Utgardaloki.

Thialfi ran as no man alive had ever run. He ran as a peregrine falcon dives, he ran as a storm wind blows, he ran like Thialfi, and nobody has ever run like Thialfi, not before and not since.

But Hugi ran on ahead easily, moving faster than ever. Before Thialfi was even halfway, Hugi had reached the end of the track and was on the way back.

"Enough!" called Utgardaloki.

They went back into the great hall. The mood among the giants was more relaxed now, more jovial.

"Ah," said Utgardaloki. "Well, the failure of these two is perhaps understandable. But now, now we shall see something to impress us. Now is the turn of Thor, god of thunder, mightiest of heroes. Thor, whose deeds are sung across the worlds. Gods and mortals tell stories of your feats. Will you show us what you can do?"

Thor stared at him. "For a start, I can drink," said Thor. "There is no drink I cannot drain."

Utgardaloki considered this. "Of course," he said. "Where is my cup-bearer?" The cup-bearer stepped forward. "Bring me my special drinking horn."

The cup-bearer nodded and walked away, returning in moments with a long horn. It was longer than any drinking horn that Thor had ever seen, but he was not concerned. He was Thor, after all, and there was no drinking horn he could not drain. Runes and patterns were engraved on the side of the horn, and there was silver about the mouthpiece.

"It is the drinking horn of this castle," said Utgardaloki. "We have all emptied it here, in our time. The strongest and mightiest of us drain it all in one go; some of us, I admit it, take two attempts to drain it. I am proud to tell you that there is nobody here so weak, so disappointing, that it has taken them three draughts to finish it."

It was a long horn, but Thor was Thor, and he raised the brimming horn to his lips and began to drink. The mead of the giants was cold and salty, but he drank it down, draining the horn, drinking until his breath gave out and he could drink no longer.

He expected to see the horn emptied, but it was as full as when he had begun to drink, or nearly as full.

"I had been led to believe that you were a better drinker than that," said Utgardaloki drily. "Still, I know you can finish it at a second draught, as we all do."

Thor took a deep breath, and he put his lips to the horn, and he drank deeply and drank well. He knew that he had to have emptied the horn this time, and yet when he lowered the horn from his lips, it had gone down by only the length of his thumb.

The giants looked at Thor and they began to jeer, but he glared at them, and they were silent.

"Ah," said Utgardaloki. "So the tales of the mighty Thor are only tales. Well, even so, we will allow you to drink the horn dry on your third attempt. There cannot be much left in there, after all."

Thor raised the horn to his lips and he drank, and he drank like a god drinks, drank so long and so deeply that Loki and Thialfi simply stared at him in astonishment.

But when he lowered the horn, the mead had gone down by only another knuckle's worth. "I am done with this," said Thor. "And I am not convinced that it is only a little mead."

Utgardaloki had his cup-bearer take away the horn. "It is time for a test of strength. Can you lift up a cat?" he asked Thor.

"What kind of a question is that? Of course I can pick up a cat."

"Well," said Utgardaloki, "we have all seen that you are not as strong as we thought you were. Youngsters here in Utgard practise their strength by picking up my housecat. Now, I should warn you, you are smaller than any of us here, and my cat is a giant's cat, so I will understand if you cannot pick her up."

"I will pick up your cat," said Thor.

"She is probably sleeping by the fire," said Utgardaloki. "Let us go to her."

The cat was sleeping, but she roused when they entered and sprang into the middle of the room. She was grey, and she was as big as a man, but Thor was mightier than any man, and he reached around the cat's belly and lifted her with both hands, intending to raise her high over his head. The cat seemed unimpressed: she arched her back, raising herself, forcing Thor to stretch up as far as he could.

Thor was not going to be defeated in a simple game of lifting a cat. He pushed and he strove, and eventually one of the cat's feet was lifted above the ground.

From far away, Thor and Thialfi and Loki heard a noise, as if of huge rocks grinding together: the rumbling noise of mountains in pain.

"Enough," said Utgardaloki. "It's not your fault that you cannot pick up my housecat, Thor. It is a large cat, and you are a scrawny little fellow at best, compared to any of our giants." He grinned.

"Scrawny little fellow?" said Thor. "Why, I'll wrestle any one of you—"

"After what we've seen so far," said Utgardaloki, "I would be a terrible host if I let you wrestle a real giant. You might get hurt. And I am afraid that none of my men would wrestle someone who could not drain my drinking horn, who could not even lift up the family cat. But I will tell you what we could do. If you wish to wrestle, I will let you wrestle my old foster mother."

"Your foster mother?" Thor was incredulous.

"She is old, yes. But she taught me how to wrestle, long ago, and I doubt she has forgotten. She is shrunken with age, so she will be closer to your height. She is used to playing with children." And then, seeing the expression on Thor's face, he said, "Her name is Elli, and I have seen her defeat men who seemed stronger than you when she wrestled them. Do not be overconfident, Thor."

"I would prefer to wrestle your men," said Thor. "But I will wrestle your old nurse."

They sent for the old woman, and she came: so frail, so grey, so wizened and wrinkled that it seemed like a breeze would blow her away. She was a giant, yes, but only a little taller than Thor. Her hair was wispy and thin on her ancient head. Thor wondered how old this woman was. She seemed older than anyone he had ever encountered. He did not want to hurt her.

They stood together, facing each other. The first to get the other one down on to the ground would win. Thor pushed the old woman and he pulled her, he tried to move her, to trip her, to force her down, but she might as well have been made of rock for all the good it did. She looked at him the whole time with her colourless old eyes and said nothing.

And then the old woman reached out and gently touched Thor on the leg. He felt his leg become less firm where she had touched him, and he pushed back against her, but she threw her arms around him and bore him towards the ground. He pushed as hard as he could, but to no avail, and soon enough he found himself forced on to one knee . . .

"Stop!" said Utgardaloki. "We have seen enough, great Thor. You cannot even defeat my old foster mother. I do not think any of my men will wrestle you now."

Thor looked at Loki, and they both looked at Thialfi. They sat beside the great fire, and the giants showed them hospitality—the food was good, and the wine was less salty than the mead from the giant's drinking horn—but each of the three of them said less than he usually would have said during a feast.

The companions were quiet and they were awkward, and humbled by their defeat.

They left the fortress of Utgard at dawn, and King Utgardaloki himself walked beside them as they left.

"Well?" said Utgardaloki. "How did you enjoy your time in my home?"

They looked up at him gloomily.

"Not much," said Thor. "I've always prided myself on being powerful, and right now I feel like a nobody and a nothing."

"I thought I could run fast," said Thialfi.

"And I've never been beaten at an eating contest," said Loki.

They passed through the gates that marked the end of Utgardaloki's stronghold.

"You know," said the giant, "you are not nobodies. And you are not nothing. Honestly, if I knew last night what I know now, I would never have invited you into my home, and I am going to make very certain you are never invited in again. You see, I tricked you, all of you, with illusions."

The travellers looked at the giant, who smiled down at them. "Do you remember Skrymir?" he asked.

"The giant? Of course."

"That was me. I used illusion to make myself so large and to change my appearance. The laces of my provision bags were tied with unbreakable iron wire and could be undone only by magic. When you hit me with your hammer, Thor, while I pretended to sleep, I knew that even the lightest of your blows would have meant my death, so I used my magic to take a mountain and put it invisibly between the hammer and my head. Look over there."

Far away was a mountain in the shape of a saddle, with valleys plunging into it: three square-shaped valleys, the last one going deepest of all.

"That was the mountain I used," said Utgardaloki. "Those valleys are your blows."

Thor said nothing, but his lips grew thin, and his nostrils flared, and his red beard prickled.

Loki said, "Tell me about last night, in the castle. Was that illusion too?"

"Of course it was. Have you ever seen wildfire come down a valley, burning everything in its path? You think you can eat fast? You will never eat as fast as Logi, for Logi is fire incarnate, and he devoured the food and the wooden trough it was in as well by burning it. I have never seen anyone eat as quickly as you."

Loki's green eyes flashed with anger and with admiration, for he loved a good trick as much as he hated being fooled.

Utgardaloki turned to Thialfi. "How fast can you think, boy?" he asked. "Can you think faster than you can run?"

"Of course," said Thialfi. "I can think faster than anything."

"Which is why I had you run against Hugi, who is thought. It does not matter how fast you ran—and none of us have ever seen anyone run like you, Thialfi—even you cannot run faster than thought."

Thialfi said nothing. He wanted to say something, to protest or to ask more questions, when Thor said, in a low rumble, like thunder echoing on a distant mountaintop, "And me? What did I actually do last night?"

Utgardaloki was no longer smiling. "A miracle," he

said. "You did the impossible. You could not perceive it, but the end of the drinking horn was in the deepest part of the sea. You drank enough to take the ocean level down, to make tides. Because of you, Thor, the seawater will rise and ebb forevermore. I was relieved that you did not take a fourth drink: you might have drunk the ocean dry.

"The cat whom you tried to lift was no cat. That was Jormungundr, the Midgard serpent, the snake who goes around the centre of the world. It is impossible to lift the Midgard serpent, and yet you did, and you even loosened a coil of it when you lifted its paw from the ground. Do you remember the noise you heard? That was the sound of the earth moving."

"And the old woman?" asked Thor. "Your old nurse? What was she?" His voice was very mild, but he had hold of the shaft of his hammer, and he was holding it comfortably.

"That was Elli, old age. No one can beat old age, because in the end she takes each of us, makes us weaker and weaker until she closes our eyes for good. All of us except you, Thor. You wrestled old age, and we marvelled that you stayed standing, that even when she took power over you, you fell down only on to one knee. We have never seen anything like last night, Thor. *Never*.

"And now that we have seen your power, we know how foolish we were to let you reach Utgard. I plan to defend my fortress in the future, and the way that I plan to defend it best is to ensure that none of you ever find Utgard, or see it again, and to be quite certain that whatever happens in the days to come, none of you will ever return."

Thor raised his hammer high above his head, but before he could strike, Utgardaloki was gone.

"Look," said Thialfi.

The fortress was gone. There was no trace of Utgardaloki's stronghold or the grounds it was in. Now the three travellers were standing on a desolate plain, with no signs of any kind of life whatsoever.

"Let's go home," said Loki. And then he said, "That was well done. Brilliantly deployed illusions. I think we've all learned something today."

"I will tell my sister that I raced thought," said Thialfi. "I will tell Roskva I ran well."

But Thor said nothing. He was thinking about the night before, and wrestling old age, of drinking the sea. He was thinking about the Midgard serpent.

THE APPLES

OF IMMORTALITY

I

This was another time that there were three of them, exploring in the mountain wastes on the edge of Jotunheim, the home of the giants. This time the three of them were Thor and Loki and Hoenir. (Hoenir was an old god. He had given the gift of reason to humans.)

Food was hard to find in those mountains, and the three gods were hungry, and getting hungrier.

They heard a noise—the lowing of distant cattle—and they looked at each other and grinned the grins of hungry men who would eat that night. They came down into a green valley, a place of life, where huge oak trees and high pine trees bordered meadows and streams, and there they saw a herd of cattle, huge and fat on the valley's grass.

They dug a pit and built a fire of wood in the pit, and they slaughtered an ox and buried it in the bed of hot coals, and they waited for the food to be done.

They opened the pit, but the meat was still raw and bloody.

Again they lit a fire. Again they waited. Again the meat had not even been warmed by the heat of the fire.

"Did you hear something?" asked Thor.

"What?" said Hoenir. "I heard nothing."

"I heard it," said Loki. "Listen."

They listened, and the sound was unmistakable. Somebody somewhere was laughing at them, vast and amused.

The three gods looked all around them, but there was no one else in the valley, only themselves and the cattle.

And then Loki looked up.

On the highest branch of the tallest tree was an eagle. It was the largest eagle that they had ever seen, a giant of an eagle, and it was laughing at them.

"Do you know why our fire will not cook our dinner?" asked Thor.

"I might know," said the eagle. "My, you do look hungry. Why don't you eat your meat raw? That is what eagles do. We tear it with our beaks. But you do not have beaks, do you?"

"We are hungry," said Hoenir. "Can you help us cook our dinner?"

"In my opinion," said the eagle, "there must be some kind of magic on your fire, draining its heat and its power. If you promise to give me some of your meat for myself, I'll give your fire back its power."

"We promise," said Loki. "You can help yourself to your portion as soon as there is cooked meat for all of us."

The eagle flew once around the meadow, beating its

wings in gusts so powerful that the coals in the pit flared and flamed and the gods were forced to hold on to each other to keep from being blown off their feet, and then it returned to its perch high in the tree.

This time they buried the meat in the firepit with a good heart, and they waited. It was the summer, when the sun barely sets in the north lands and the day lasts forever, so it was late in the night that still felt like day when they opened the pit, to be met with the glorious smell of cooked beef, tender and ready for their knives and their teeth.

As the pit was opened, the eagle swooped down and seized in its claws the two rear haunches of the ox, along with a shoulder, and began to tear at it with a ravenous beak. Loki was furious, seeing much of his dinner about to be devoured, and he struck at the eagle with his spear, hoping to force it to drop its plundered food.

The eagle flapped its wings hard, creating a wind so strong it almost knocked the gods over, and it dropped the meat. Loki had no time to enjoy his triumph, because, he discovered, the spear was stuck in the great bird's side, and as the eagle took off into the air, it carried him with it.

Loki wanted to let go of his spear, but his hands were stuck to the shaft. He could not let go.

The bird flew low, so Loki's feet were dragged over stones and gravel, over mountainside and over trees. There was magic at work, and it was a magic mightier than anything Loki could control.

"Please!" he shouted. "Stop this! You are going to tear my arms from my sockets. My boots are already destroyed. You are going to kill me!"

The eagle soared off the side of a mountain and circled gently in the air, with only the crisp air between them and the ground. "Perhaps I will kill you," it said.

"Whatever it takes to make you put me down," gasped Loki. "Whatever you want. Please."

"I want," said the eagle, "Idunn. And I want her apples. The apples of immortality."

Loki hung in the air. It was a long way down.

Idunn was married to Bragi, god of poetry, and she was sweet and gentle and kind. She carried a box with her, made of ash wood, which contained golden apples. When the gods felt age beginning to touch them, to frost their hair or ache their joints, then they would go to Idunn. She would open her box and allow the god or goddess to eat a single apple. As they ate it, their youth and power would return to them. Without Idunn's apples, the gods would scarcely be gods . . .

"You are not saying anything. I think," said the eagle, "I will drag you over some more rocks and mountaintops. Perhaps I will also drag you through some deep rivers this time."

"I'll get the apples for you," said Loki. "I swear it. Just let me down."

The eagle said nothing, but with a twitch of a wing it began to descend to a green meadow from which a fire's smoke rose. A swoop, down to where Thor and Hoenir were standing open-mouthed, looking up at them. As the eagle flew above the firepit, Loki found himself falling, still grasping his spear, and he tumbled on to the grass. With a cry, the eagle beat its wings and rose above them, and in moments it was a tiny dot in the sky.

"I wonder what that was about," said Thor.

"Who knows?" said Loki.

"We left you some food," said Hoenir.

Loki had lost his appetite, which his friends attributed to his flight in the air.

Nothing else interesting or out of the ordinary occurred on their way home.

II

The next day Idunn was walking through Asgard, greeting the gods, looking at their faces to see if any of them were beginning to look old. She passed Loki. Normally Loki ignored her, but this morning he smiled at her and greeted her.

"Idunn! So good to see you! I feel age upon me," he told her. "I need to taste one of your apples."

"You do not look as if you are ageing," she said.

"I hide it well," said Loki. "Oh! My aching back. Old age is a terrible thing, Idunn."

Idunn opened her ash-wood box and gave Loki a golden apple.

He ate it with enthusiasm, devouring it, seeds and all. Then he made a face.

"Oh dear," he said. "I thought you'd have, well, nicer apples than this."

"What a peculiar thing to say," said Idunn. Never before had her apples been received like this. Normally gods talked only about the perfection of the flavour and how good it was to feel young again. "Loki, they are the apples of the gods. The apples of immortality."

Loki looked unconvinced. "Perhaps," he said. "But I saw some apples in the forest that were finer in every way than your apples. Looked nicer, smelled nicer, tasted nicer than these. I think they were apples of immortality too. Perhaps a better kind of immortality than yours."

He watched expressions chasing each other across Idunn's face—disbelief, puzzlement, and concern.

"These are the only apples like this that there are," she said.

Loki shrugged. "I'm just telling you what I saw," he said.

Idunn walked beside him. "Where are these apples?" she asked.

"Over there. Not sure I could tell you how to get there, but I could take you through the forest. It's not a long walk."

She nodded.

"But when we see the apple tree," said Loki, "how will we be able to compare those apples to the ones in your ash box back in Asgard? I mean, I could say, they are even better than your apples, and you would say, nonsense, Loki, these are shrivelled crab apples compared to my apples, and how could we tell?"

"Don't be silly," said Idunn. "I will bring my apples. We will compare them."

"Oh," said Loki. "What a clever idea. Well, then. Let's go."

He led her into the forest, Idunn holding tightly to her ash box containing the apples of immortality.

After half an hour of walking, Idunn said, "Loki, I am starting to believe that there are no other apples and there is no apple tree."

"That's unkind of you, and hurtful," said Loki. "The apple tree is just at the top of that hill there."

They walked up to the top of the hill. "There is no apple tree here," said Idunn. "Only that tall pine, with the eagle in it."

"Is that an eagle?" asked Loki. "It's very big."

As if it heard them, the eagle spread its wings and dropped from the pine tree.

"No eagle am I," said the eagle, "but the giant Thiazi in eagle shape, here to claim the beautiful Idunn. You will be a companion to my daughter, Skadi. And perhaps you will learn to love me. But whatever happens, time and immortality have run out for the gods of Asgard. So say I! So says Thiazi!"

It seized Idunn in one taloned claw and the ash-wood

box of apples in the other, and it rose into the sky above Asgard and was gone.

"So that's who that was," said Loki to himself. "I knew it wasn't just an eagle." And he made his way home, hoping vaguely that nobody would notice that Idunn and her apples were gone, or that if they did, it would be long after anyone would connect her disappearance with Loki taking Idunn into the forest.

III

"You were the last to see her," said Thor, rubbing the knuckles of his right hand.

"No, I wasn't," said Loki. "Why would you even say that?"

"And you haven't become *old* like the rest of us," said Thor.

"I'm old but I'm lucky," said Loki. "I wear it well."

Thor grunted, entirely unconvinced. His red beard was now snow-white with a few pale orange hairs in it, like a once-proud fire become white ashes.

"Hit him again," said Freya. Her hair was long and grey, and the lines in her face were deep and careworn. She was still beautiful, but it was the beauty of age, not of a golden-haired maiden. "He knows where Idunn is. And he knows where the apples are." The necklace of the Brisings still hung around her neck, but it was dull and tarnished, and it did not shine.

Odin, father of the gods, held on to his staff with knobby, arthritic fingers, blue-veined and twisted. His voice, always booming and commanding, was now cracked and dusty. "Do not hit him, Thor," he said in his old voice.

"See? I knew that you at least would see reason, All-father," said Loki. "I had nothing to do with it! Why would Idunn have gone anywhere with me? She didn't even like me!"

"Do not hit him," repeated Odin, and he peered at Loki with his one good eye, now glaucous grey. "I want him to be whole and unbroken when he is tortured. They are heating the fires now, and sharpening the blades, and collecting the rocks. We may be old, but we can torture and we can kill as well as ever we could when we were in our prime and had the apples of Idunn to keep us young."

The smell of burning coals reached Loki's nostrils.

"If . . ." he said. "If I manage to work out what happened to Idunn, and if I were somehow to bring her and her apples back to Asgard safely, could we forget all about the torture and death?"

"It is your only chance at life," said Odin, in a voice so old and cracked that Loki could not tell whether it was the voice of an old man or an old woman. "Bring Idunn back to Asgard. And the apples of immortality."

Loki nodded. "Unfasten these chains," he told them. "I'll do it. I'll need Freya's falcon-feather cloak, though."

"My cloak?" asked Freya.

"I'm afraid so."

Freya walked stiffly away and returned with a cloak covered with falcon feathers. Loki's chains were unfastened, and he reached for the cloak.

"Don't think you can just fly off and never return," said Thor, and he stroked his white beard meaningfully. "I may be old now," he said, "but if you do not return, ancient as I am, I will hunt you down, wherever you hide, and I and my hammer will be your death. For I am still Thor! And I am still strong!"

"You are still extremely irritating," said Loki. "Save your breath, and you can use your strength in making a pile of wood shavings beyond the walls of Asgard. An enormous pile of wood shavings. You will need to cut down many trees and chip them into thin shavings. I'll need a long high pile, along the wall, so you should start now."

Then Loki wrapped the falcon cloak tightly about himself and, in falcon form, flapped his wings and rose, faster even than an eagle, and was gone, flying north, towards the lands of the frost giants.

IV

Loki flew in the shape of a falcon without pause until, deep in the lands of the frost giants, he reached the fortress of the giant Thiazi, and he perched on the high roof, observing all that went on beneath.

He watched Thiazi, in giant form, lumber out of his keep and walk across the shingle to a rowing boat bigger than the largest whale. Thiazi hauled the boat down the strand into the cold waters of the northern ocean and rowed with huge strokes out into the sea. Soon he was lost to sight.

Then Loki flew as a falcon about the keep, peering into each window as he went. In the farthest room, through a barred window, he saw Idunn, sitting and weeping, and he perched on the bars.

"Cease your weeping!" he said. "It is I, Loki, here to rescue you!"

Idunn glared at him with red-rimmed eyes. "It is you who are the source of my troubles," she said.

"Well, perhaps. But that was so long ago. That was yesterday's Loki. Today's Loki is here to save you and to take you home."

"How?" she asked.

"Do you have the apples with you?"

"I am a goddess of the Aesir," she told him. "Where I am, the apples also are." She showed him the box of apples.

"That makes things simple," said Loki. "Close your eyes."

She closed her eyes, and he transformed her into a hazelnut in its shell, with the green husk still clinging to it. Loki closed his talons on the nut, hopped up to and between the bars of the window, and began the journey home.

Thiazi had a poor day's fishing. No fish were biting for him. He decided that the best use of his time would be to return to his keep and pay court to Idunn. He would tease her by telling her just how, with her and her apples gone, all the gods were frail and withered—drooling, palsied, quivering hulks, slow of thought and crippled in mind and body. He rowed home to his keep and went at a run to Idunn's room.

It was empty.

Thiazi saw a falcon's feather on the ground, and he knew in that moment where Idunn was and who had taken her.

He leapt into the sky in the form of an eagle even huger and mightier than any he had been before, and he began to beat his wings and flew, faster and ever faster, towards Asgard.

The world moved beneath him. The wind blew about him. He went even faster, so fast that the air itself boomed with the sound of his passing.

Thiazi flew onwards. He left the land of the giants and entered the land of the gods. When he spotted a falcon ahead of him, Thiazi let out a scream of rage and increased his speed.

The gods of Asgard heard the screech and the boom of the wings, and they went to the high walls to see what was happening. They saw the little falcon coming towards them, the enormous eagle so close behind it. The falcon was so close . . .

"Now?" asked Thor.

"Now," said Freya.

Thor set fire to the wood shavings. There was a moment before they caught—a moment just long enough for the falcon to fly over them and to settle inside the castle, and then, with a *whoomph*, they burst into flame. It was like an eruption, a gout of fire higher than the walls of Asgard itself: terrifying, and unimaginably hot.

Thiazi in eagle form could not stop himself, could not slow his flight, could not change direction. He flew into the flames. The giant's feathers caught fire, the tips of his wings burned, and, a featherless eagle, he fell from the air and crashed into the ground with a bang and a thud that shook the fortress of the gods.

Burned, dazed, stunned, the naked eagle was no match even for elderly gods. Before he could transform himself back into giant shape he was already wounded, and as he changed from bird into giant, a blow of Thor's hammer parted Thiazi from his life.

V

Idunn was glad to be reunited with her husband. The gods ate of the apples of immortality and regained their youth. Loki hoped that the matter was now done with.

It wasn't. Thiazi's daughter, Skadi, put on her armour, picked up her weapons, and came to Asgard to avenge her father.

"My father was everything to me," she said. "You killed him. His death fills my life with tears and misery. I have no joy in my life. I am here for vengeance, or for compensation."

The Aesir and Skadi bargained for compensation, back and forth. In those days, each life had a price on it, and Thiazi's life was priced highly. When the negotiations were concluded, the gods and Skadi had agreed that she would be recompensed for her father's death in three ways.

First, that she would be given a husband, to take the place of her dead father. (It was obvious to all the gods and goddesses that Skadi had set her heart on Balder, the most beautiful of all the gods. She kept winking at him and staring until Balder would look away, blushing and embarrassed.)

Second, that the gods would make her laugh again, because she had not smiled or laughed since her father had been killed.

And last, that the gods would make it so that her father would never be forgotten.

The gods let her choose a husband from their number, but they had one condition: they told her that she could not choose her husband by seeing his face. The male gods would all stand behind a curtain, with only their feet showing. Skadi would have to choose her husband by his feet.

One by one the gods walked past the curtain, and

Skadi stared at their feet. "Ugly feet," she would say as each set of feet went past.

Then she stopped, and exclaimed with delight, "Those are the feet of my husband-to-be!" she said. "Those are the most beautiful feet! They must be Balder's feet— nothing on Balder could be ugly."

And while Balder was indeed beautiful, the feet she had chosen, Skadi discovered when the curtain was lifted, belonged to Njord, god of chariots, father of Frey and of Freya.

She married him then and there. At the wedding feast that followed her face was the saddest any of the Aesir had ever seen.

Thor nudged Loki. "Go on," he said. "Make her laugh. This is all your fault anyway."

Loki sighed. "Really?"

Thor nodded, and he tapped the handle of his hammer meaningfully.

Loki shook his head. Then he went outside, to pens where the animals were kept, and he came back into the wedding feast leading a large, extremely irritated billy goat. Loki irritated the goat even more by tying a strong rope tightly around its beard.

Then Loki tied the other end of the rope around his own private parts.

He tugged on the rope with his hand. The goat screamed, feeling its beard tugged painfully, and it jerked back. The rope pulled hard on Loki's private parts. Loki screamed and grabbed for the rope again, yanking it back.

The gods laughed. It did not take a lot to make the gods laugh, but this was the best thing they had seen in a long time. They placed bets on what would be torn off first, the goat's beard or Loki's private parts. They mocked Loki for screaming. "Like a fox wailing in the night-time!" exclaimed Balder, stifling his laughter. "Loki sounds like a weeping baby!" giggled Balder's brother, Hod, who was blind but still laughed every time Loki screeched.

Skadi did not laugh, although the ghost of a smile began to haunt the corners of her lips. Every time the goat screamed or Loki wailed like a child in pain, her smile became a little wider.

Loki pulled. The goat pulled. Loki screamed and yanked the rope. The goat yelped and pulled back even harder.

The rope snapped.

Loki shot through the air, clutching at his groin, and landed smack in Skadi's lap, whimpering and broken.

Skadi laughed like an avalanche in mountain country. She laughed as loudly as a calving glacier. She laughed so long and hard that tears of laughter glittered in her eyes, and as she laughed, for the first time she reached out and squeezed her new husband Njord's hand.

Loki clambered down from her lap and staggered away, both hands clutching between his legs as he went, glaring in an aggrieved fashion at all the gods and goddesses, who only laughed the louder.

"We are done, then," said Odin, the all-father, to Skadi, the giant's daughter, when the wedding feast was over. "Or almost done."

He signalled Skadi to follow him out into the night, and she and Odin walked out of the hall together, with her new husband by her side. Beside the funeral pyre the gods had made for the remains of the giant, two huge orbs sat, filled with light.

"Those orbs," said Odin to Skadi, "those were your father's eyes."

The all-father took the two eyes and threw them up into the night sky, where they burned and glittered together, side by side.

Look up into the night in midwinter. You can see them there, twin stars, one blazing beside the other. Those two stars are Thiazi's eyes. They are shining still.

THE STORY OF

GERD AND FREY

I

Frey, the brother of Freya, was the mightiest of the Vanir. He was handsome and noble, a warrior and a lover, but he was missing something in his life, and he did not know what it was.

The mortals of Midgard revered Frey. He made the seasons, they said. Frey made the fields fertile and brought forth life from the dead ground. The people worshipped Frey and they loved him, but this did not fill the empty place inside him.

Frey took stock of his possessions:

He had a sword so powerful and remarkable that it fought by itself. But this did not satisfy Frey.

He had Gullinbursti, the boar with the golden bristles, created by the dwarf Brokk and his brother, Eitri. Gullinbursti pulled Frey's chariot. It could run through the air and over the water, run faster than any horse, and run even in the darkest night, for its golden bristles shone so brightly. But Gullinbursti did not satisfy Frey.

He had *Skiðblaðnir*, a boat made for him by the three

dwarfs known as the sons of Ivaldi. It was not the biggest ship there was (that was *Naglfar*, the Death Ship, made from the untrimmed fingernails of the dead), but there was room for all of the Aesir on board. When the sails of *Skiðblaðnir* were set, the winds were always fair, and it took you wherever you needed to go. Even though it was the second biggest ship there had ever been and would hold all the Aesir, Frey could fold *Skiðblaðnir* up like a cloth and place it in his bag. It was the best of all ships. But *Skiðblaðnir* did not satisfy him.

He owned the finest residence that was not Asgard. It was Alfheim, the home of the light elves, where he was always welcomed and acknowledged as overlord. There was nowhere like Alfheim, and yet it did not satisfy him.

Frey's servant, Skirnir, was one of the light elves. He was the finest of servants, wise of counsel and fair of face.

Frey ordered Skirnir to harness Gullinbursti, and they set out for Asgard together.

When they reached Asgard, they walked towards Valhalla, the great hall of the slain. In Odin's Valhalla live the Einherjar, "those who fight alone"—all the men who have died nobly in battle since the beginning of time. Their souls are taken from the battlefields by Valkyries, the warrior women charged by Odin with the task of bringing the souls of the noble dead, battle-slain, to their ultimate reward.

"There must be a lot of them," said Skirnir, who had not been there before.

"There are," Frey told him. "But there are more to come. And still more will be needed when we fight the wolf."

They heard the sound of battle as they approached the fields around Valhalla; they heard the clash of metal on metal, the thud of metal on flesh.

As they watched, they saw powerful warriors of all ages and places, well matched in battle, dressed in their war gear, each man fighting his hardest. Soon enough half the men were lying dead on the grass.

"Enough," called a voice. "The battle is over for the day!"

At this, those who were still standing helped the dead men get up from the courtyard floor. Their wounds healed as Frey and Skirnir watched, and they clambered on to their horses. All the soldiers who had fought that day, whether they had won or lost, rode home to Valhalla, the hall of the noble dead.

Valhalla was an enormous hall. It had 540 doors, and each door allowed 800 warriors to walk abreast. It seated more people than the mind could hold.

In the hall, the warriors cheered as the feast began. They were eating boar meat, ladled out from an enormous cauldron. This was the meat of the boar Saerimnir: every night they would feast upon the boar's meat, and each morning the monstrous beast would be alive again, ready to be slain later that day and to give its life and its flesh to feed the noble dead. No matter how many of them there were, there would always be enough meat.

Mead was brought for them to drink.

"So much mead for so many warriors," said Skirnir. "Where does it come from?"

"It comes from a goat called Heidrun," Frey told him. "She stands on top of Valhalla and eats the leaves of the tree called Lerad, which is what we call that branch of Yggdrasil, the world-tree. From her udders the finest mead flows. There will always be enough for every warrior."

They walked to the high table, where Odin sat. He had a bowl of meat in front of him but did not taste it. He would stab a piece of meat with his knife from time to time and flick it on to the ground, to be eaten by one of his wolves, Geri and Freki.

Two ravens sat on Odin's shoulders, and he would give the ravens scraps of meat as well, while they whispered to him of things that were happening far away.

"He isn't eating," whispered Skirnir.

"He does not need to," said Frey. "He drinks. He only needs wine, nothing else. Come on. We are done here."

"Why were we here?" asked Skirnir as they walked out of one of the 540 doors of Valhalla.

"Because I wanted to make certain that Odin was here in Valhalla with the warriors and not in his own hall at the Hlidskjalf, the observation point."

They entered Odin's hall. "Wait here," said Frey.

Frey walked alone into Odin's hall and clambered up on to the Hlidskjalf, the throne from which Odin could see everything that happened across the nine worlds.

Frey looked out across the worlds. He looked to the south, to the east, and to the west, and he did not see the thing he was looking for.

And then he looked to the north and saw the thing he was missing in his life.

Skirnir was waiting by the door when his master came from the hall. There was an expression on Frey's face Skirnir had never seen before, and Skirnir was afraid.

They left that place without speaking.

II

Frey drove the chariot pulled by Gullinbursti back to his father's hall. Frey spoke to nobody when they got there, neither his father, Njord, who is the master of all who sail the seas, nor his stepmother, Skadi, the lady of the mountains. He went to his room with a face as dark as midnight, and there he stayed.

On the third day, Njord sent for Skirnir.

"Frey has been here for three days and three nights," Njord said. "He has not eaten, nor has he drunk anything."

"This is true," said Skirnir.

"What have we done to anger him so?" asked Njord. "My son, who was always so gentle and filled with kind, wise words, now says nothing, only looks at us with fury. What did we do to upset him so?"

"I do not know," said Skirnir.

"Then," said Njord, "you must go to him and ask him

what is happening. Ask him why he is so angry he will not speak to any of us."

"I would rather not," said Skirnir. "But I cannot refuse you, lord. He is in such a strange, dark mood, I am afraid of what he will do if I ask him."

"Ask him," said Njord. "And do what you can for him. He is your master."

Skirnir of the light elves went to where Frey stood looking out at the sea. Frey's face was clouded and troubled, and Skirnir hesitated to approach him.

"Frey?" said Skirnir.

Frey said nothing.

"Frey? What has happened? You are angry. Or you are downcast. Something has happened. You have to tell me what is happening to you."

"I am being punished," said Frey, and his voice sounded hollow and distant. "I went to the all-father's holy seat, and I looked out at the world. For my arrogance in believing I had a right to the observation place, my happiness has been taken from me forever. I have paid for my crime, and I am paying still."

"My lord," said Skirnir, "what did you see?"

Frey was silent, and Skirnir thought he had once again sunk into a troubled silence. But after some time he said, "I looked to the north. I saw a dwelling there, a splendid house. And I saw a woman walking up to the house. I have never seen a woman like her. Nobody who looks like her. Nobody who moves like her. As she raised her arms to unlock the door to her house, the light glanced off her arms, and it seemed to illuminate the air and to brighten the sea, and because she is in it, the whole world is a brighter and more beautiful place. And then I looked away and saw her no more, and my world became dark and hopeless and empty."

"Who is she?" asked Skirnir.

"A giant. Her father is Gymir the earth giant, her mother a mountain giant, Aurboda."

"And does this beautiful creature have a name?"

"Her name is Gerd." Frey was silent once more.

Skirnir said, "Your father is worried about you. We are all worried. Is there something I can do?"

"If you will go to her and ask for her hand, I would give anything. I cannot live without her. Bring her back to me, to be my wife, whatever her father says. I will pay you so well."

"You are asking a lot, my lord," said Skirnir.

"I will give anything," said Frey fervently, and he shivered.

Skirnir nodded. "I will do this thing, lord." He hesitated. "Frey, may I look at your sword?"

Frey took out his sword and held it out for Skirnir to examine. "There is no other sword like this. It will fight by itself, without a hand holding it. It will always protect you. No other sword, no matter how powerful, can penetrate its defense. They say that this sword could even prevail against the flaming sword of Surtr, the fire demon."

Skirnir shrugged. "It is a fine sword. If you wish me to bring you Gerd, this sword will be my wages."

Frey nodded assent. He gave Skirnir his sword, and a horse to ride.

Skirnir travelled north until he reached the house of Gymir. He entered as a guest and explained who he was and who had sent him. He told the beautiful Gerd of his master, Frey. "He is the most splendid of all the gods," he told her. "He has dominion over the rain and the weather and the sunshine, and he gives the folk of Midgard good harvests and peaceful days and nights. He watches over the prosperity and abundance of humanity. All people love and worship him."

He told Gerd of the beauty of Frey, and of his power. He told her of the wisdom of Frey. And at the last he told her of the love Frey bore for her, how he had been heart-struck by a vision of her and now would no longer eat or sleep, drink or speak, until she agreed to be his bride.

Gerd smiled, and her eyes shone with joy. "Tell him yes," she said. "I will meet him on the isle of Barri for the wedding, nine days from now. Go and tell him."

Skirnir returned to Njord's hall.

Before he could even climb down from his horse, Frey was there, even more pale and even more wan than when he had left him. "What news?" he asked. "Do I rejoice, or do I despair?"

"She will take you to be her husband nine days from now, on the island of Barri," said Skirnir.

Frey looked at his servant without joy. "The nights without her in my life last forever," he said. "One night is so long. Two nights are even longer. How will I manage to cope with three nights? Four days feel like a month to me, and you expect me to wait nine days?"

And Skirnir looked at his lord with pity.

Nine days from that day, on the isle of Barri, Frey and Gerd met for the first time, and they married in a field of waving barley. She was as beautiful as he had dreamed, and her touch was as fine, her kiss as sweet, as he had hoped. Their wedding was blessed, and some say that their son, Fjolnir, went on to become the first king of Sweden. (He would drown in a vat of mead late one night, hunting in the darkness for a place to piss.)

Skirnir took the sword he had been given, Frey's sword that fought all by itself, and he returned to Alfheim with it.

The beautiful Gerd filled the hole in Frey's life, and the hole in his heart. Frey did not miss his sword, and he did not replace it. When he fought the giant Beli, he killed him with a stag's antler. Frey was so strong, he could kill a giant with his bare hands.

Even so, he should not have given his sword away.

Ragnarok is coming. When the sky splits asunder and the dark powers of Muspell march out on their war journey, Frey will wish he still had his sword.

HYMIR AND THOR'S FISHING EXPEDITION

The gods arrived at Aegir's huge hall at the edge of the sea. "We are here," called Thor, who was at the head of the company. "Make a feast for us!"

Aegir was the greatest of the sea giants. His wife was Ran, into whose net those who drown at sea are gathered. His nine daughters are the waves of the sea.

Aegir had no desire to feed the gods, but he also had no wish to fight them. He looked Thor in the eye and said, "I will make a banquet, and it will be the finest feast that any of you will ever have attended. My servant, Fimafeng, will serve each of you diligently, bringing you as much food as your bellies can hold, as much ale as you can drink. I have only one condition: I will throw the feast, but you must first bring me a cauldron big enough to brew ale for you all. There are so many of you, and your appetites are huge."

Aegir knew well that the gods had no such cauldron. And without the cauldron, he did not have to give the feast.

Thor asked the other gods for advice, but each god he asked was of the opinion that such a cauldron did not exist. Finally he asked Tyr, god of battle, god of war. Tyr scratched his chin with his left hand, which was his only hand. "On the edge of the world sea," he said, "lives the giant king Hymir. He owns a cauldron three miles deep. It's the biggest cauldron there has ever been."

"Can you be sure?" asked Thor.

Tyr nodded. "Hymir is my stepfather. He is married to my mother," he said. "She is a giant. I have seen the great cauldron with my own eyes. And as my mother's son, I will be welcome in Hymir's hall."

Tyr and Thor climbed into Thor's chariot, pulled by the goats Snarler and Grinder, and swiftly they travelled to Hymir's enormous fortress. Thor tied the goats to a tree, and the two made their way inside.

There was a giantess in the kitchen, cutting up onions as big as boulders and cabbages the size of boats. Thor could not help staring: the old woman had nine hundred heads, each head uglier and more terrifying than the last. He took a step backwards. If Tyr was disturbed, he did not show it. Tyr called out, "Greetings, Grandmother. We are here to see if we can borrow Hymir's cauldron to brew our beer."

"Such tiny things! I thought you were mice," said Tyr's grandmother, and when she spoke it sounded like a crowd of people shouting. "You do not want to talk to me, Grandson. You should talk to your mother."

She called out, "We have guests! Your son is here, with a friend," and in moments another giantess walked in. This was Hymir's wife, Tyr's mother. She was dressed in golden cloth, and she was as beautiful as her mother-in-law was alarming; she carried two of the tiniest giant thimbles, which she had filled with beer. Thor and Tyr gripped the thimbles, which were the size of buckets, and they drank the beer with enthusiasm.

It was excellent beer.

The giantess asked Thor his name. Thor was about to tell her, but before he could speak Tyr said, "His name is Veor, Mother. He's my friend. And an enemy of the enemies of Hymir and the giants."

They heard a distant rumbling, like thunder on the peaks, or mountains crumbling, or huge waves crashing to shore, and the earth shook with each rumble.

"My husband is coming home," said the giantess. "I hear his gentle footsteps in the distance."

The rumbling became more distinct and seemed to be coming rapidly closer.

"My husband is often bad-tempered when he gets home, wrathful and grim of mind. He treats his guests badly," the giantess warned them. "Why don't you get under that kettle and stay there until he's cheerful enough for you to come out?"

She hid them beneath a kettle on the floor of the kitchen. It was dark under there.

The ground shook, a door slammed, and Thor and Tyr

knew that Hymir must be home. They heard the giant-ess tell her husband that they had guests, her son and a friend, and that he had to be on his best behaviour as a gracious host and not kill them.

"Why?" The giant's voice was loud and petulant.

"The little one is our son, Tyr. You remember him. The big one's name is Veor. Be nice to him."

"*Thor*? Thor our enemy? Thor who has killed more giants than anyone else, even other giants? Thor whom I have sworn to slay if ever I encounter him? Thor the—"

"Veor," said his wife, calming him down. "Not Thor. *Veor*. He's our son's friend, and an enemy of your enemies, so you have to be nice to him."

"I am grim of mind and wrathful of spirit and I have no desire to be nice to anyone," said a huge rumbling giant's voice. "Where are they hiding?"

"Oh, just behind that beam over there," said his wife.

Thor and Tyr heard a crash as the beam she had pointed to was smashed and broken. This was followed by another series of crashes as, one after another, all the kettles in the kitchen were knocked down from the ceil-ing and destroyed.

"Are you finished breaking things?" asked Tyr's mother.

"I suppose so," said Hymir's voice grudgingly.

"Then look under that kettle," she said. "The one on the floor that you didn't destroy."

The kettle beneath which Tyr and Thor were hidden was lifted, and they found themselves staring up at an enormous face, its features twisted into a sulky scowl. This, Thor knew, was Hymir, the giant king. His beard was like a forest of ice-covered trees in midwinter, his eyebrows like a field of thistles, his breath as rank and foul as a midden in a bog.

"Hello, Tyr," said Hymir, without enthusiasm.

"Hello, Father," said Tyr, with, if possible, even less pleasure.

"You will join us as guests at dinner," said Hymir. He clapped his hands.

The door of the hall opened, and a giant ox was led in, its coat shining, its eyes bright, its horns sharp. It was followed by another, even more beautiful, and then the last ox, even finer than the first two.

"These are the most excellent oxen in existence. So much bigger and fatter than the beasts of Midgard or Asgard. I am," Hymir confided, "enormously proud of my herd of cattle. They are my treasures, and the delight of my eyes. I treat them like my own children." And for a moment his scowling face seemed to soften.

The grandmother with nine hundred heads killed each ox, skinned it, and tossed it into her enormous cooking pot. The pot boiled and bubbled over a fire which hissed and spat, and she stirred it with a spoon as big as an oak tree. She sang quietly to herself as she cooked, in a voice like a thousand old women all singing at the tops of their voices at once.

Soon enough the food was ready.

"You are guests here. Do not stand on ceremony. Take as much as you can eat from the pot," said Hymir expansively. The strangers were small, after all—how much could they eat? After all, the oxen were enormous.

Thor said he didn't mind if he did, and he proceeded to devour two of the oxen all by himself, one after the other, leaving nothing but clean-picked bones. Then he belched in a satisfied way.

"That's a lot of food, Veor," said Hymir. "It was meant to feed us for several days. I do not think I have ever seen even a giant eat two of my oxen at once before."

"I was hungry," said Thor. "And I got a little carried away. Look, tomorrow, why don't we go out fishing? I hear you are quite a fisherman."

Hymir prided himself on his skills at fishing. "I am an excellent fisherman," he said. "We can catch tomorrow night's dinner."

"I too am a fine fisherman," said Thor. He had never fished before, but how hard could it be?

"We'll meet tomorrow at dawn, out on the dock," said Hymir.

In their huge bedroom that night, Tyr said to Thor, "I hope you know what you are doing."

"Of course I do," said Thor. But he didn't. He was just doing whatever he felt like doing. That was what Thor did best.

In the grey light before dawn, Thor met Hymir on the dock.

"I should warn you, little Veor," said the giant, "that we will be going far out into the icy waters. I row farther out into the cold and stay out longer than a tiny thing like you can survive. Icicles will form on your beard and your hair, and you will turn blue with cold. Probably you will die."

"Doesn't worry me," said Thor. "I like the cold. It's bracing. What are we using for bait?"

"I already have my own bait," said Hymir. "You must find your own. You could look in the field of the oxen for it. Nice big maggots in the ox dung, after all. Bring whatever you want from there."

Thor looked at Hymir. He thought about hitting Hymir with his hammer, but then he would never get the cauldron, not without a fight. He walked back up the shore.

In the meadow was Hymir's herd of beautiful oxen. There were giant patties of dung on the ground, with huge maggots writhing and burrowing in them, but Thor avoided all of them. Instead he walked over to the biggest, most majestic, fattest of the beasts, raised his fist, and thumped it between the eyes, killing it instantly.

Thor ripped off the beast's head, placed it in his sack, and carried it down to the sea.

Hymir was in the boat. He had already cast off and was rowing out of the bay.

Thor jumped into the cold water and swam out, hauling his sack behind him. He grabbed the back of the boat with numb fingers, then hauled himself onboard, dripping with seawater, ice crusting his red beard.

"Ah," said Thor. "That was fun. Nothing to wake you up on a cold morning like a good swim."

Hymir said nothing. Thor took the other set of oars, and they began to row together. Soon enough the land was gone and they were alone on the waters of the northern sea. The ocean was grey, the waves were choppy and high, and the wind and the seagulls screamed.

Hymir stoppped rowing. "We will fish here," he said.

"Here?" asked Thor. "We've hardly gone out into the sea at all." And he picked up the oars and began single-handedly to row them into deeper waters.

The boat flew across the waves.

"Stop!" boomed Hymir. "These waters are dangerous. This is where Jormungundr, the Midgard serpent, is to be found."

Thor stopped rowing.

Hymir took two large fish from the bottom of the boat. He gutted them with his sharp, sharp bait knife, tossed the guts into the sea, then impaled the fish on the hooks of his line.

Hymir dropped his baited fishing line. He waited until the line jerked and twitched in his hand, and then he hauled up the line: two monstrous whales hung from it, the hugest whales that Thor had ever seen. Hymir grinned with pride.

"Not bad," said Thor.

He pulled the head of the ox from his sack. When Hymir saw the dead eyes of his favourite ox, his face froze.

"I got bait," said Thor helpfully. "From the ox field. Like you said." Expressions of shock, of horror and of anger chased each other across Hymir's huge face, but he said nothing.

Thor took Hymir's fishing line, rammed the ox's head on to the hook, and threw the line and the head into the ocean. He felt it sink to the bottom.

He waited.

"Fishing," he said to Hymir. "I suppose it must all be about learning patience. It's a bit dull, isn't it? I wonder what I'm going to catch for our dinner."

And that was when the sea erupted. Jormungundr, the Midgard serpent, had bitten down on the huge ox head, and the hook had dug deep into the roof of its mouth. The serpent writhed in the water, trying to free itself.

Thor held on to the line.

"It's going to drag us under!" boomed Hymir in horror. "Let go of the line!"

Thor shook his head. He strained against the fishing line, determined to hold on.

The thunder god slammed his feet through the bottom of the boat, and he used the sea bottom to brace himself, and he began to haul Jormungundr up on board.

The serpent spat gouts of black poison towards them. Thor ducked, and the poison missed him. He continued to pull.

"It's the Midgard serpent, you fool!" shouted Hymir. "Let go of the line! We'll both die!"

Thor said nothing, just hauled the line in, hand over hand, his eyes fixed on his enemy. "I will kill you," he whispered to the serpent, beneath the roar of the waves and the howl of the wind and the thrashing and screaming of the beast. "Or you will kill me. This I swear."

He said it beneath his breath, but he could have sworn that the Midgard serpent heard him. It fixed him with its eyes, and the next gout of poison came so close to Thor that he could taste it on the ocean air. The poison sprayed his shoulder, and it burned where it touched.

Thor simply laughed and hauled again.

Somewhere, it seemed to Thor, in the distance, Hymir was babbling and grumbling and shouting about the monstrous serpent, and about the sea rushing into the rowing boat through the holes in the bottom, and about how they would both die out here, in the cold, cold ocean, so far from dry land. Thor did not care about any of this. He was fighting the serpent, playing it, letting it exhaust itself thrashing and pulling.

Thor began to pull the fishing line back on to the boat.

The Midgard serpent's head was almost within striking distance. Thor reached down without glancing away, and his fingers closed around the haft of his hammer. He knew just where the head of the hammer would need to strike to kill the serpent. One more heave on the fishing line and—

Hymir's bait knife flashed, and the line was cut. Jormungundr, the serpent, reared up, high above the boat, then tumbled back into the sea.

Thor threw his hammer at it, but the monster was already gone, vanished into the cold grey waters. The hammer returned, and Thor caught it. He turned his attention back to the sinking fishing boat. Hymir was desperately bailing the water from the bottom.

Hymir bailed the water, and Thor rowed the boat back to shore. The two whales that Hymir had caught earlier, at the prow of the boat, made the rowing harder than it normally would have been.

"There's the shore," gasped Hymir. "But my home is still many miles distant."

"We could make land here," said Thor.

"Only if you are willing to carry the boat and me and the two whales I caught all the way to my hall," said Hymir, exhausted.

"Mm. All right."

Thor jumped over the side of the fishing boat. A few moments later, Hymir felt the boat rising into the air. Thor was carrying them on his back: boat, oars, Hymir and whales, carrying them along the shingle at the edge of the sea.

When they reached Hymir's hall, Thor lowered the boat to the ground.

"There," said Thor. "I brought you home, as you requested. Now I need a favour from you in return."

"What is it?" asked Hymir.

"Your cauldron. The huge one you brew beer in. I want to borrow it."

Hymir said, "You are a mighty fisherman, and you row hard. But you are asking for the finest brewing kettle in existence. The beer that is magically brewed in it is the best of beers. I will only lend it to someone who can break the cup I drink from."

"That doesn't sound very hard," said Thor.

They ate roast whale meat for dinner that night, in a hall filled with many-headed giants, all of them shouting and happy and most of them drunk. After they had eaten, Hymir drained the last of the beer from his drinking cup and called for silence. Then he handed the cup to Thor.

"Smash it," he said. "Smash this cup, and the cauldron in which I brew my beer is yours as my gift to you. Fail and you die."

Thor nodded.

The giants stopped their joking and their songs. They watched him warily.

Hymir's fortress was built of stone. Thor took the drinking cup, hefted it in both hands, then threw it with all his might against one of the granite pillars that held up the roof of the banqueting hall. There was an ear-splitting crash, and the air was filled with blinding dust.

When the dust settled, Hymir got up and walked over to what was left of the granite pillar. The cup had gone through first one pillar, then another, breaking them into tiny fragments of stone. In the rubble of the third pillar was the drinking cup, a little dusty but quite undamaged.

Hymir held his drinking cup above his head, and the

giants cheered and laughed and made faces at Thor with all their heads, along with crude gestures.

Hymir sat down at the table once more. "See?" he said to Thor. "I didn't think you were strong enough to break my cup." He held up the cup, and his wife poured beer into it. Hymir slurped the beer. "Best beer you will ever taste," he said. "Here, wife, pour more beer for your son and for his friend Veor. Let them taste the best beer there is and be sad that they will not be taking my cauldron home with them, and that they will never again taste beer this good. Also, they will be sad that I need to kill Veor now, for my cup remains unbroken."

Thor sat at the table beside Tyr and picked up a lump of charred whale meat and chewed it resentfully. The giants were raucous and loud, and now were ignoring him.

Tyr's mother leaned over to fill Thor's cup with beer. "You know," she said quietly, "my husband has a very hard head. He's stubborn and thick-skulled."

"They say the same of me," said Thor.

"No," she said, as if she were talking to a small child. "He has a *very* hard head. Hard enough to break even the toughest of cups."

Thor drained his beer. It really was the best beer he had ever tasted. He stood up and walked over to Hymir. "Can I try again?" he asked.

The giants in the hall all laughed at this, and none of them laughed louder than Hymir.

"Of course you can," he said.

Thor picked up the drinking cup. He faced the stone wall, hefted the cup once, twice, then turned swiftly on his heel and smashed the cup down on Hymir's forehead.

The fragments of the cup fell one by one on to Hymir's lap.

There was silence in the hall then, a silence broken by a strange heaving noise. Thor looked around to see what the noise was, and then he turned back and saw Hymir's shoulders shaking. The giant was crying, in huge, heaving sobs.

"My greatest treasure is no longer mine," said Hymir. "I could always tell it to brew me ale, and the cauldron itself would magically brew the finest beer. Never again will I say, 'Brew me ale, my cauldron.'"

Thor said nothing.

Hymir looked at Tyr and said bitterly, "If you want it, stepson, then take it. It's huge and heavy. It takes over a dozen giants to lift it. Do you think you are strong enough?"

Tyr walked over to the cauldron. He tried to lift it once, twice, but it was too heavy even for him. He looked at Thor. Thor shrugged, grasped the cauldron by the rim, and flipped it so he was inside it and the handles clattered at his feet.

Then the cauldron began to move, with Thor inside. It headed towards the door, while all around the hall many-headed giants stared, open-mouthed.

Hymir no longer wept. Tyr glanced up at him. "Thank

you for the cauldron," he said. And then, keeping the moving cauldron between himself and Hymir, Tyr edged out of the room.

Thor and Tyr left the castle together, untethered Thor's goats, and climbed into Thor's chariot. Thor still carried the cauldron on his back. The goats ran as best they could, but while Snarler ran well and ran fast, even with the weight of the giant's cauldron to pull, Grinder limped and staggered. Its leg had once been broken for marrow, and Thor had set it, but the goat had never been as strong again.

Grinder bleated in pain as it ran.

"Can't we go any faster?" asked Tyr.

"We can try," said Thor, and he whipped the goats so they ran even faster.

Tyr looked behind. "They are coming," he said. "The giants are coming."

They were indeed coming, with Hymir at their rear, urging them on: all the giants of that part of the world, a many-headed monstrous bunch, the giants of the waste, misshapen and deadly. An army of giants, all intent on getting their cauldron back.

"Go faster!" said Tyr.

It was then that the goat called Grinder stumbled and fell, throwing them out of the chariot.

Thor staggered to his feet. Then he threw the cauldron to the ground and began to laugh.

"What are you laughing about?" asked Tyr. "There are hundreds of them."

Thor hefted Mjollnir, his hammer. "I didn't catch and kill the serpent," he said. "Not *this* time. But a hundred giants almost make up for it."

Methodically, enthusiastically, one after the next, Thor killed the giants of the waste, until the earth ran black and red with their blood. Tyr fought one-handed, but he fought bravely, and he slew his share of giants that day.

When they were done and all the giants were dead, Thor crouched beside Grinder, his injured goat, and helped it back to its feet. The goat limped as it walked, and Thor cursed Loki, whose fault it was that his goat was lame. Hymir was not among the slain, and Tyr was relieved, for he did not want to bring his mother any additional distress.

Thor carried the cauldron to Asgard, to the meeting of the gods.

They took the cauldron to Aegir. "Here," said Thor. "A brewing cauldron big enough for all of us."

The sea giant sighed. "It is indeed what I asked for," he said. "Very well. There will be an autumn feast for all the gods in my hall."

He was as good as his word, and since then, every year once the harvest is in, the gods drink the finest ale there ever was or will be, in the autumn, in the sea giant's hall.

THE DEATH
OF BALDER

I

Nothing there is that does not love the sun. It gives us warmth and life; it melts the bitter snow and ice of winter; it makes plants grow and flowers bloom. It gives us the long summer evenings, when the darkness never comes. It saves us from the bitter days of midwinter, when the darkness is broken for only a handful of hours and the sun is cold and distant, like the pale eye of a corpse.

Balder's face shone like the sun: he was so beautiful that he illuminated any place he entered. Balder was Odin's second son, and he was loved by his father, and by all things. He was the wisest, the mildest, the most eloquent of all the Aesir. He would pronounce judgement, and all would be impressed by his wisdom and his fairness. His home, the hall called Breidablik, was a place of joy and music and knowledge.

Balder's wife was Nanna, and he loved her and only her. Their son, Forsete, was growing to become as wise a judge as his father. There was nothing wrong with Balder's life or his world, save only one thing.

Balder had bad dreams.

He dreamed of worlds ending, and of the sun and the moon being eaten by a wolf. He dreamed of pain and death without end. He dreamed of darkness, of being trapped. Brothers slew brothers in his dreams, and nobody could trust anyone else. In his dreams, a new age would come upon the world, an age of storm and of murder. Balder would wake from these dreams in tears, troubled beyond all telling.

Balder went to the gods and he told them of his nightmares. None of them knew what to make of the dreams, and they too were troubled, all but one of them.

When Loki heard Balder talk of his bad dreams, Loki smiled.

Odin set out to find the cause of his son's dreams. He put on his grey cloak and his broad-brimmed hat, and when folk asked his name, he said he was Wanderer, son of Warrior. Nobody knew the answers to his questions, but they told him of a seer, a wise woman, who understood all dreams. She could have helped him, they said, but she was long dead.

At the end of the world was the wise woman's grave. Beyond it, to the east, was the realm of the dead who had not died in battle, ruled over by Hel, Loki's daughter by the giantess Angrboda.

Odin travelled east, and he stopped when he reached the grave.

The all-father was the wisest of the Aesir, and he had given his eye for more wisdom.

He stood by the grave at the end of the world, and in that place he invoked the darkest of runes and called on old powers, long forgotten. He burned things, and he said things, and he charmed and he demanded. The storm wind whipped at his face, and then the wind died and a woman stood before him on the other side of the fire, her face in the shadows.

"It was a hard journey, coming back from the land of the dead," she told him. "I've been buried here for such a long time. Rain and snow have fallen on me. I do not know you, man-who-raised-me. What do they call you?"

"They call me Wanderer," said Odin. "Warrior was my father. Tell me the news from Hel."

The dead wise woman stared at him. "Balder is coming to us," she told him. "We are brewing mead for him. There will be despair in the world above, but in the world of the dead there will be only rejoicing."

Odin asked her who would kill Balder, and her answer shocked him. He asked who would avenge Balder's death, and her answer puzzled him. He asked who would mourn Balder, and she stared at him across her own grave, as if she were seeing him for the first time.

"You are not Wanderer," she said. Her dead eyes flickered, and there was expression on her face. "You are Odin, who was sacrificed by himself to himself so long ago."

"And you are no wise woman. You are she who was in life Angrboda, Loki's lover, mother to Hel, to Jormungundr, the Midgard serpent, and to Fenris Wolf," said Odin.

The dead giantess smiled. "Ride home, little Odin,"

she told him. "Run away, run back to your hall. No one will come to see me now until my husband, Loki, escapes from his bonds and returns to me, and Ragnarok, the doom of the gods, tearing all asunder, approaches."

And then there was nothing in that place but shadows.

Odin left with his heart heavy, and with much to think about. Even the gods cannot change destiny, and if he was to save Balder he would have to do it with cunning, and he would need help. There was one other thing that the dead giantess had said that disturbed him.

Why did she talk about Loki escaping his bonds? wondered Odin. *Loki is not bound.* And then he thought, *Not yet.*

II

Odin kept his own counsel, but he told Frigg, his wife, mother of the gods, that Balder's dreams were true dreams, and that there were those who meant their favourite son harm.

Frigg thought. Practical as ever, she said, "I do not believe it. I shall not believe it. There is nothing that despises the sun and the warmth and the life it brings the earth, and by the same token there is nothing that hates my son Balder the beautiful." And she set out to ensure that this was so.

She walked the earth and exacted an oath from each thing that she encountered never to harm Balder the beautiful. She spoke to fire, and it promised it would not burn him; water gave its oath never to drown him; iron would not cut him, nor would any of the other metals. Stones promised never to bruise his skin. Frigg spoke to trees, to beasts, and to birds and to all things that creep and fly and crawl, and each creature promised that its kind would never hurt Balder. The trees agreed, each after its kind, oak and ash, pine and beech, birch and fir, that their wood could never be used to hurt Balder. She conjured diseases and spoke to them, and each of the diseases and infirmities that can hurt or wound a person agreed that it too would never touch Balder.

Nothing was too insignificant for Frigg to ask, save only the mistletoe, a creeping plant that lives on other trees. It seemed too small, too young, too insignificant, and she passed it by.

And when everything had sworn its oath not to harm her son, Frigg returned to Asgard. "Balder is safe," she told the Aesir. "Nothing will hurt him."

All of them doubted her, even Balder. Frigg picked up a stone and whipped it towards her son. The stone skipped around him.

Balder laughed with delight, and it was as if the sun had come out. The gods smiled. And then one by one they threw their weapons at Balder, and each of them was astonished and amazed. Swords would not touch him, spears would not pierce his flesh.

All the gods were relieved and happy. There were only two faces in Asgard that were not radiant with joy.

Loki was not smiling or laughing. He watched the gods hack at Balder with axes and with swords, or drop enormous rocks on Balder, or try to strike Balder with huge knotted wooden clubs, and laugh as the clubs and swords and rocks and axes avoided Balder or touched him like gentle feathers, and Loki brooded, and slipped away into the shadows.

The other was Balder's brother Hod, who was blind.

"What is happening?" asked blind Hod. "Will somebody please tell me what is happening?" But nobody talked to Hod. He listened to the sound of merrymaking and joy, and he wished he could be a part of it.

"You must be very proud of your son," said a kindly woman to Frigg. Frigg did not recognise the woman, but the woman beamed when she looked at Balder, and Frigg was indeed proud of her son. Everybody loved him, after all. "But won't they hurt him, the poor darling? Throwing things at him like that? If I were his mother, I would be afraid for my son."

"They will not hurt him," said Frigg. "No weapon can hurt Balder. No disease. No rock. No tree. I have taken an oath from all the things there are that can harm."

"That's good," said the kindly woman. "I'm pleased. But are you sure you didn't miss any of them?"

"Not a one," said Frigg. "All the trees. The only one I did not bother with was the mistletoe—it's a creeper that grows on the oak trees west of Valhalla. But it's too young and too small ever to do any harm. You could not make a club from mistletoe."

"My, my," said the kindly woman. "Mistletoe, eh? Well,

truth to tell, I wouldn't have bothered with that either. Much too weedy."

The kindly woman had begun to remind Frigg of someone, but before the goddess could think who it was, Tyr held up an enormous rock with his good left hand, held it high above his head, and crashed it down on Balder's chest. It disintegrated into dust before ever it touched the shining god.

When Frigg turned back to talk to the kindly woman, she was already gone, and Frigg thought no more about it. Not then.

Loki, in his own form, travelled to the west of Valhalla. He stopped by a huge oak tree. Here and there pendulous clumps of green mistletoe leaves and pale white berries hung from the oak, seeming even more insignificant when seen next to the grandeur of the oak. They grew directly out of the bark of the oak tree. Loki examined the berries, the stems and the leaves. He thought about poisoning Balder with mistletoe berries, but that seemed too simple and straightforward.

If he was going to do harm to Balder, he was going to hurt as many people as possible.

III

Blind Hod stood to one side, listening to the merriment and the shouts of joy and astonishment coming from the green, and he sighed. Hod was strong, even if he was sightless, one of the strongest of the gods, and usually Balder was good about making certain that he was included. This time, even Balder had forgotten him.

"You look sad," said a familiar voice. It was Loki's voice.

"It's hard, Loki. Everyone is having such a good time. I hear them laughing. And Balder, my beloved brother, he sounds so happy. I just wish I could be part of it."

"That is the easiest thing in the world to remedy," said Loki. Hod could not see the expression on his face, but Loki sounded so helpful, so friendly. And all the gods knew that Loki was clever. "Hold out your hand."

Hod did so. Loki put something into it, closed Hod's fingers around it.

"It is a little wooden dart I made. I will bring you close to Balder, and I will point you at him, and you shall throw it at him as hard as you can. Throw it with all your might. And then all the gods will laugh and Balder will know that even his blind brother has taken part in his day of triumph."

Loki walked Hod through the people, towards the hubbub. "Here," said Loki. "This is a good place to stand. Now, when I tell you, throw the dart."

"It is only a little dart," said Hod wistfully. "I wish I were throwing a spear or a rock."

"A little dart will do," said Loki. "The tip of it is sharp enough. Now, throw it there, like I told you."

A mighty cheer and a laugh: a club made of knotted thornbush wood studded with sharp iron nails was swung by Thor into Balder's face. The club skipped up and over his head at the last moment, and Thor looked as if he were dancing. It was very comical.

"Now!" whispered Loki. "Now, while they are all laughing."

Hod threw the dart of mistletoe, just as he had been told. He expected to hear cheers and laughter. Nobody laughed, and nobody cheered. There was silence. He heard gasps, and a low muttering.

"Why is nobody cheering me?" asked blind Hod. "I threw a dart. It was neither big nor heavy, but you must have seen it. Balder, my brother, why are you not laughing?"

He heard wailing then, high and keen and awful, and he knew the voice. It was his mother who wailed.

"Balder, my son. Oh Balder, oh my son," she wailed.

It was then that Hod knew his dart had hit home.

"How terrible. How sad. You have killed your brother," said Loki. But he did not sound sad. He did not sound sad at all.

IV

Balder lay dead, pierced by the mistletoe dart. The gods gathered, weeping and tearing their garments. Odin said nothing, save only, "No vengeance will be taken on Hod. Not yet. Not right now. Not at this time. We are in a place of holy peace."

Frigg said, "Who among you wants to win my good graces by going to Hel? Perhaps she will let Balder return to this world. Even Hel could not be so cruel as to keep him . . ." She thought for a moment. Hel was, after all, Loki's daughter. "And we will offer her a ransom to give us Balder back. Is there one of you who is willing to travel to Hel's kingdom? You might not return."

The gods looked at each other. And then one of them raised his hand. This was Hermod, called the Nimble, Odin's attendant, the fastest and the most daring of the young gods.

"I will go to Hel," he said. "I will bring back Balder the beautiful."

They brought forth Sleipnir, Odin's stallion, the eight-legged horse. Hermod mounted it and prepared to ride down, ever down, to greet Hel in her high hall, where only the dead go.

As Hermod rode into darkness, the gods prepared Balder's funeral. They took his corpse and they placed it on *Hringhorn*, Balder's ship. They wanted to launch the ship and burn it, but they could not move it from the shore. They all pushed and heaved, even Thor, but the ship sat on the shore, unmoving. Only Balder had been able to launch his ship, and now he was gone.

The gods sent for Hyrrokkin the giantess, who came to them riding on an enormous wolf, with serpents for reins. She went to the prow of Balder's ship and she pushed as hard as she could: she launched the ship, but her push was so violent that the rollers the ship was on burst into flame, and the earth shook, and the waves were terrifying.

"I ought to kill her," said Thor, still stinging from his own failure to launch the ship, and he grasped the handle of Mjollnir, his hammer. "She shows disrespect."

"You will do nothing of the kind," said the other gods.

"I'm not happy about any of this," said Thor. "I'm going to kill somebody soon, just to relieve the tension. You'll see."

Balder's body was brought down the shingle, borne by four gods; eight legs took him past the crowd assembled there. Odin was foremost in the crowd of mourners, his ravens on each shoulder, and behind him the Valkyries and the Aesir. There were frost giants and mountain giants at Balder's funeral; there were even dwarfs, the cunning craftsmen from beneath the ground, for all things that there were mourned the death of Balder.

Balder's wife, Nanna, saw her husband's body carried past. She wailed, and her heart gave out in her breast, and she fell dead on to the shore. They carried her to the funeral pyre, and they placed her body beside Balder's. Out of respect, Odin placed his arm-ring Draupnir on to the pyre; this was the miraculous ring made for him by the dwarfs Brokk and Eitri, which every nine days would drip eight other rings of equal purity and beauty. Then Odin whispered a secret into Balder's dead ear, and what Odin whispered none but he and Balder will ever know.

Balder's horse, fully caparisoned, was ridden to the pyre and sacrificed there, in order that it would be able to bear its master in the world to come.

They lit the pyre. It burned, consuming the body of Balder and the body of Nanna, and his horse, and his possessions.

Balder's body flamed like the sun.

Thor stood in front of the funeral pyre, and he held Mjollnir high. "I sanctify this pyre," he proclaimed, darting grumpy looks at the giantess Hyrrokkin, who still did not, Thor felt, appear to be properly respectful.

Lit, one of the dwarfs, walked in front of Thor to get a better view of the pyre, and Thor kicked him irritably into the middle of the flames, which made Thor feel slightly better and made all the dwarfs feel much worse.

"I don't like this," said Thor testily. "I don't like any of it one little bit. I hope Hermod the Nimble is sorting things out with Hel. The sooner Balder comes back to life, the better it will be for all of us."

V

Hermod the Nimble rode for nine days and nine nights without stopping. He rode deeper and he rode through gathering darkness: from gloom to twilight to night to a pitch-black starless dark. All that he could see in the darkness was something golden glinting far ahead of him.

Closer he rode, and closer, and the light grew brighter.

It was gold, and it was the thatch of the bridge across the Gjaller River, across which all who die must travel.

He slowed Sleipnir to a walk as they crossed the bridge, which swung and shook beneath them.

"What is your name?" asked a woman's voice. "Who are your kin? What are you doing in the land of the dead?"

Hermod said nothing.

He reached the far end of the bridge, where a maiden stood. She was pale and very beautiful, and she looked at him as if she had never seen anything like him before. Her name was Modgud, and she guarded the bridge.

"Yesterday enough dead men to fill five kingdoms crossed this bridge, but you alone cause it to shake more than they did, though there were men and horses beyond all counting. I can see the red blood beneath your skin. You are not the colour of the dead—they are grey, and green, and white, and blue. Your skin has life beneath it. Who are you? Why are you travelling to Hel?"

"I am Hermod," he told her. "I am a son of Odin, and I am riding to Hel on Odin's horse to find Balder. Have you seen him?"

"No one who saw him could ever forget it," she said. "Balder the beautiful crossed this bridge nine days ago. He went to Hel's great hall."

"I thank you," said Hermod. "That is where I also must go."

"It is downwards, and northwards," she told him. "Always

go down, and keep travelling north. You will reach Hel's gate."

Hermod rode on. He rode northerly, and he followed the path down until he saw before him a huge high wall and the gates to Hel, which were higher than the tallest tree. Then he dismounted from his horse, and he tightened the girth strap. He remounted, and holding tight to the saddle, he urged Sleipnir faster and faster, and at the last it leapt, a jump like no horse has made before or since, and it cleared the gates of Hel and landed safely upon the other side, in Hel's domain, where no living person can ever go.

Hermod rode to the great hall of the dead, dismounted, and walked inside. Balder, his brother, was seated at the head of the table, at the seat of honour. Balder was pale; his skin was the colour of the world on a grey day, when there is no sun. He sat and drank the mead of Hel, and ate her food. When he saw Hermod he told him to sit beside him and spend the night with them at the table. On the other side of Balder was Nanna, his wife, and next to her, and not in the best of tempers, was a dwarf called Lit.

In Hel's world, the sun never rises and the day can never begin.

Hermod looked across the hall, and he saw a woman of peculiar beauty. The right side of her body was the colour of flesh, but the left-hand side of her body was dark and ruined, like that of a week-old corpse that you might find hanging from a tree in the forest or frozen into the snow, and Hermod knew that this was Hel, Loki's daughter, whom the all-father had set to rule over the lands of the dead.

"I have come for Balder," said Hermod to Hel. "Odin himself sent me. All things there are mourn him. You must give him back to us."

Hel was impassive. One green eye stared at Hermod, and one sunken, dead eye. "I am Hel," she said simply. "The dead come to me, and they do not return to the lands above. Why should I let Balder go?"

"All things mourn him. His death unites us all in misery, god and frost giant, dwarf and elf. The animals mourn him, and the trees. Even the metals weep. The stones dream that brave Balder will return to the lands that know the sun. Let him go."

Hel said nothing. She watched Balder with her mismatched eyes. And then she sighed. "He is the most beautiful thing, and, I think, the best thing, ever to come to my realm. But if it is truly as you say, if all things mourn Balder, if all things love him, then I will give him back to you."

Hermod threw himself at her feet. "That is noble of you. Thank you! Thank you, great queen!"

She looked down at him. "Get up," she said. "I have not said I will give him back. This is your task, Hermod. Go and ask them. All the gods and the giants, all the rocks and the plants. Ask everything. If all things in the world weep for him and want him to return, I will give Balder back to the Aesir and the day. But if one creature will not cry or speaks against him, then he stays with me forever."

Hermod got to his feet. Balder led him from the hall, and he gave Hermod Odin's ring, Draupnir, to return to Odin, as evidence that Hermod had been to Hel. Nanna gave him a linen robe for Frigg and a golden ring for Fulla, Frigg's handmaiden. Lit just grimaced and made rude gestures.

Hermod clambered back on Sleipnir. This time the gates of Hel were opened for him, as he left, and he retraced his steps. He crossed the bridge, and eventually he saw daylight once again.

In Asgard Hermod returned the arm-ring Draupnir to Odin, the all-father, and told him all that had happened and all that he had seen.

While Hermod was in the underworld, Odin had had a son to replace Balder; this son, named Vali, was the son of Odin and the goddess Rind. Before he was a day old, the baby found and slew Hod. So Balder's death was avenged.

VI

The Aesir sent messengers across the world. The messengers of the Aesir rode like the wind, and they asked each thing they encountered if it wept for Balder, so that Balder could be free of Hel's world. The women wept, and the men, the children, and the animals. Birds of the air

wept for Balder, as did the earth, the trees, the stones—
even the metals the messengers encountered wept for
Balder, in the way that a cold iron sword will weep when
you take it from the freezing cold into the sunlight and
warmth.

All things wept for Balder.

The messengers were returning from their mission,
triumphant and overjoyed. Balder would soon be back
among the Aesir.

They rested on a mountain, on a ledge beside a cave,
and they ate their food and drank their mead, and they
joked and they laughed.

"Who is that?" called a voice from inside the cave,
and an elderly giantess came out. There was something
vaguely familiar about her, but none of the messengers
was entirely certain what it was. "I am Thokk," she said,
which means "gratitude". "Why are you here?"

"We have asked each thing there is if it would weep for
Balder, who is dead. Beautiful Balder, killed by his blind
brother. For each of us misses Balder as we would miss
the sun in the sky, were it never to shine again. And each
of us weeps for him."

The giantess scratched her nose, cleared her throat and
spat on to the rock.

"Old Thokk won't weep for Balder," she said bluntly.
"Alive or dead, old Odin's son brought me nothing but
misery and aggravation. I'm glad he's gone. Good rid-
dance to bad rubbish. Let Hel keep him."

Then she shuffled back into the darkness of her cave and was lost to sight.

The messengers returned to Asgard and told the gods what they had seen, and that they had failed in their mission, for there was one creature that did not weep for Balder and did not want him to return: an old giantess in a cave on a mountain.

And by then they had also realised who old Thokk reminded them of: she had moved and talked much like Loki, the son of Laufey.

"I expect it was really Loki in disguise," said Thor. "Of course it was Loki. It's always Loki."

Thor hefted his hammer, Mjollnir, and gathered a group of the gods to go looking for Loki, to take their revenge, but the crafty troublemaker was nowhere to be seen. He was hiding, far from Asgard, hugging himself in glee at his own cleverness and waiting for the fuss to die away.

THE LAST DAYS
OF LOKI

I

Balder was dead, and the gods were still mourning his loss. They were sad, and the grey rains fell unceasingly, and there was no joy in the land.

Loki, when he returned from one of his journeys to distant parts, was unrepentant.

It was the time of autumn feast in Aegir's hall, where the gods and elves were gathered to drink the sea giant's fresh-brewed ale, brewed in the cauldron Thor had brought back from the land of the giants so long ago.

Loki was there. He drank too much of Aegir's ale, drank himself beyond joy and laughter and trickery and into a brooding darkness. When Loki heard the gods praise Aegir's servant, Fimafeng, for his swiftness and diligence, he sprang up from the table and stabbed Fimafeng with his knife, killing him instantly.

The horrified gods drove Loki out of the feast hall, into the darkness.

Time passed. The feasting continued, but now it was subdued.

There was a commotion at the doorway, and when the gods and goddesses turned to find out what was happening, they saw that Loki had returned. He stood in the entry to the hall staring at them, with a sardonic smile on his face.

"You are not welcome here," said the gods.

Loki ignored them. He walked up to where Odin was sitting. "All-father. You and I mixed our blood long, long ago, did we not?"

Odin nodded. "We did."

Loki smiled even more widely. "Did you not swear back then, great Odin, that you would drink at a banqueting table only if Loki, your sworn blood brother, drank with you?"

Odin's good grey eye stared into Loki's green eyes, and it was Odin who looked away.

"Let the wolf's father feast with us," said Odin gruffly, and he made his son Vidar move over to make room for Loki to sit down beside him.

Loki grinned with malice and delight. He called for more of Aegir's ale and gulped it down.

One by one that night Loki insulted the gods and the goddesses. He told the gods that they were cowards, told the goddesses that they were gullible and unchaste. Each insult was woven with just enough truth to make it wound. He told them that they were fools, reminded them of things they thought were safely forgotten. He sneered and jeered and raised old scandals, and would not stop making everyone there miserable until Thor arrived at the feast.

Thor ended the conversation very simply: he threatened to use Mjollnir to shut Loki's evil mouth for good and send him to Hel, all the way to the hall of the dead.

Loki left the feast then, but before he swaggered out, he turned to Aegir. "You brewed fine ale," said Loki to the sea giant. "But there will never be another autumn feast here. Flames will take this hall; your skin will be burned from your back by the fire. Everything you love will be taken from you. This I swear."

And he walked away from the gods of Asgard, into the dark.

II

Loki sobered up the next morning and thought about what he had done the night before. He felt no shame, for shame was not Loki's way, but he knew that he had pushed the gods too far.

Loki had a home on a mountain near the sea, and decided to wait there until the gods had forgotten him. He had a house on the top of the mountain with four doors, one on each side, allowing him to see danger coming towards him from any direction.

During the day Loki would transform himself into a salmon, and he would hide in the pool at the bottom of Franang's Falls, a high waterfall that tumbled down the mountainside. A stream connected the pool to a little river, and the river led directly to the sea.

Loki liked plans and counterplans. As a salmon he was fairly safe, he knew. The gods themselves could not catch salmon as they swam.

But then he began to doubt himself. He wondered, *Could there be a way of catching a fish in the deep waters of the pool beneath the waterfall?*

How would he, the craftiest of all, the most cunning planner, catch a salmon?

Loki took a ball of nettle yarn, and he began to knot and weave it into a fishing net, the first such net ever to be made. *Yes*, he thought. *If I used this net, I could catch a salmon.*

Now, he thought, *to work out a counterplan: what will I do if the gods weave a net like this one?*

He examined the net he had made.

Salmon can jump, he thought. *They can swim upstream, even travel up waterfalls. I could jump over the net.*

Something drew his attention. He peered out from first one door and then another. He was startled: the gods were coming up the mountainside, and they had almost reached his house.

Loki flung the net into the fire and watched it burn with satisfaction. Then he stepped into Franang's Falls. In the shape of a silver salmon, Loki was swept over the waterfall, and he vanished into the depths of the deep pool at the base of the mountain.

The Aesir reached Loki's house on the mountain. They waited by each door, cutting off Loki's escape, if he was still inside.

Kvasir, wisest of the gods, walked in through the first door. Once he had been dead, and mead had been brewed from his blood, but now he was alive once more. He could tell from the fire and from the half-drunk cup of wine beside it that Loki had been there only moments before he arrived.

There was no clue to where Loki could have gone, though. Kvasir scanned the sky. Then he looked down at the floor and at the fireplace.

"He's gone, the snivelling little weasel," said Thor, coming in through another of the four doors. "He could have transformed himself into anything. We'll never find him."

"Do not be so hasty," said Kvasir. "Look."

"It's only ashes," said Thor.

"But look at the pattern of it," said Kvasir. He bent down, touched the ash on the floor beside the fire, sniffed it, then touched it to his tongue. "It is the ash of a cord that has been thrown into the fire and burned. Cord just like that ball of nettle twine in the corner."

Thor rolled his eyes. "I do not think that the ashes of a burned cord are going to tell us where Loki is."

"You think not? But look at the pattern—a criss-cross diamond shape. And the squares are perfectly regular."

"Kvasir, you are wasting all our time admiring the shapes that the ash makes. This is foolishness. Every moment we spend staring at the ash is time in which Loki is getting farther and farther away."

"Perhaps you are right, Thor. But to make the squares in the cord that regular, you would need something to space them with, like that piece of scrap wood on the floor by your foot. You would need to tie one end of the cord to something as you wove it—something like that stick jutting from the floor over there. Then you would knot and thread your rope, weaving it, so that one piece of cord would form a . . . hmm. I wonder what Loki called it. I will call it a *net*."

"Why are you still jabbering?" said Thor. "Why are you staring at ash and at sticks and scraps of wood when we could be chasing Loki? Kvasir! As you ponder and talk your nonsense he is getting away from us!"

"I think that such a net as this would be best used to trap fish," said Kvasir.

"I am done with you and your foolishness," sighed Thor. "So it's to be used to trap fish? Well, bully for you. Loki would have been hungry, and so he must have wanted to catch fish to eat. Loki invents things. That's what he does. He always was clever. That's why we used to keep him around."

"You are correct. But ask yourself, why would you, if you were Loki, invent something to trap fish with, and then throw the net you made on to the fire when you knew we were coming?"

"Because . . ." said Thor, creasing his brow and pondering so hard that distant thunder could be heard in the mountaintops. "Er . . ."

"Exactly. Because you would not want us to find it when we arrived. And the only reason for not wanting us to find it is to stop us, the gods of Asgard, from using it to trap you."

Thor nodded slowly. "I see," he said. Then, "Yes, I suppose so," he said. And finally, "So Loki . . ."

". . . is hiding in the deep water pool at the foot of the waterfall, in the shape of a fish. Yes, exactly! I knew you would get there in the end, Thor."

Thor nodded with enthusiasm, not entirely certain how he had come to this conclusion from ashes on the floor but happy to know where Loki was hiding.

"I will go down there, to the pool, with my hammer," said Thor. "And I will . . . I will . . ."

"We will need to go down there with a net," said Kvasir, the wise god.

Kvasir took the remaining nettle twine and the piece of spacing wood. He tied the end of the twine to the stick, and he began to wrap the twine around the stick, to weave it in and around and through. He showed the other gods what he was doing, and soon each of them was weaving and knotting. He attached the nets they made one to the other until they had a net as long as the pool, and they made their way down the side of the waterfall to the base of the mountain.

There was a stream that ran out of the pool where it overflowed. That stream ran down towards the sea.

When they reached the base of Franang's Falls, the gods unrolled the net they had made. The net was huge and heavy, and long enough to go from one end of the pool to the other. It took all the warriors of the Aesir to hold up one end of it and Thor to hold up the other end.

The gods started from one end of the pool, beginning immediately underneath the falls and wading until they reached the other side. They caught nothing.

"There's definitely something living down there," said Thor. "I felt it push against the net. But it swam down deeper, into the mud, and the net went over it."

Kvasir scratched his chin thoughtfully. "Not a problem. We need to do it again, but this time we will weigh down the bottom of the net," he said. "So nothing can get underneath it."

The gods gathered heavy stones with holes in them and tied each stone to the bottom of the net as a weight.

The gods waded into the pool again.

Loki had been pleased with himself the first time the gods had entered his pool. He had simply swum down to the muddy bottom of the pool, slipped between two flat stones, and waited while the net had gone above him.

Now he was worried. Down in the dark and the cold, he thought about this.

He could not transform himself into something else until he left the water, and even if he did, the gods would be after him. No, it was safer to remain in salmon shape. But as a salmon he was trapped. He would have to do what the gods would not be expecting. They would expect him to head for the open sea—he would be safe there, if he got to the sea, even if he would be easy to spot and catch in the river that led from the pool to the bay.

The gods would not expect him to swim back the way he had come. Up the waterfall.

The gods hauled their net along the bottom of the pool.

They were intent upon what was happening in the depths, and so were taken by surprise when a huge silver fish, bigger than any salmon they had ever seen before, leapt over the net with a twist of its tail and began swimming upstream. The huge salmon swam up the falls, springing up and defying gravity as if it had been thrown upwards into the air.

Kvasir shouted at the Aesir, ordering them to form into two groups, one on one end of the net, one on the other.

"He will not stay in the waterfall for long. It's too exposed. His only chance is still to make it to the sea. So you two groups will walk along, dragging the net between you. Meanwhile, Thor," said Kvasir, who was wise, "you will wade in the middle, and when Loki tries that jumping-over-the-net trick again, you must snatch him from the air, like a bear catching a salmon. Do not let him go, though. He is tricky."

Thor said, "I have seen bears pluck leaping salmon from the air. I am strong, and I am as fast as any bear. I will hold on."

The gods began to drag the net upstream, towards the

place where the huge silver salmon was biding its time. Loki planned and plotted.

As the net came closer, Loki knew that this was the critical moment. He had to leap the net as he had done before, and this time he would race towards the sea. He tensed, like a spring about to whip back, and then he shot into the air.

Thor was fast. He saw the silver salmon glitter in the sun, and he grabbed it with his huge hands, just as a hungry bear snatches a salmon from the air. Salmon are slippery fish, and Loki was the slipperiest of salmon; he wriggled and tried to slip through Thor's fingers, but Thor simply gripped the fish harder and squeezed it tightly, down by the tail.

They say that salmon have been narrower near the tail ever since.

The gods brought their net, and they wrapped it tightly around the fish and carried it between them. The salmon began to drown in the air, gasping for water, and then it thrashed and twitched, and now they were carrying a panting Loki.

"What are you doing?" he asked. "Where are you taking me?"

Thor just shook his head and grunted, and did not reply. Loki asked the other gods, but none of them would tell him what was happening, and none of them would meet his eye.

III

The gods entered the mouth of a cave, and with Loki slung between them, they went down deep into the earth. Stalactites hung from the ceiling of the cave, and bats fluttered and flickered. They went down lower. Soon the way was too narrow to carry Loki, and now they let him walk between them. Thor walked immediately behind Loki, his hand on Loki's shoulder.

They went down a long, long way.

In the deepest of the caves there were brands burning, and three people stood there, waiting for them. Loki recognised them before he saw their faces, and his heart sank. "No," he said. "Do not hurt them. They did nothing wrong."

Thor said, "They are your sons and your wife, Loki Lie-Smith."

There were three huge flat stones in that cave. The Aesir set each stone on its side, and Thor took his hammer. He broke a hole through the middle of each stone.

"Please! Let our father go," said Narfi, Loki's son.

"He is our father," said Vali, Loki's other son. "You have sworn oaths that you will not kill him. He is a blood brother and an oath brother to Odin, highest of the gods."

"We will not kill him," said Kvasir. "Tell me, Vali, what is the worst thing that one brother could do to another?"

"For a brother to betray his brother," said Vali, without hesitating. "For a brother to murder a brother, as Hod killed Balder. This is abominable."

Kvasir said, "It is true that Loki is a blood brother to the gods, and we cannot kill him. But we are bound by no such oaths to you, his sons."

Kvasir spoke words to Vali, words of change, words of power.

Vali's human shape fell from him, and where Vali had stood was a wolf, foam flecking its muzzle. The intelligence of Vali was fading from its yellow eyes, to be replaced by hunger, by anger, by madness. It looked at the gods, at Sigyn, who had been its mother, and finally it saw Narfi. It growled low and long in the back of its throat, and its hackles rose.

Narfi took a step back, only a step, and then the wolf was on him.

Narfi was brave. He did not scream, not even when the wolf that had been his brother tore him apart, ripping open his throat and spilling his guts on to the rock floor. The wolf that had been Vali howled once, long and loudly, through blood-soaked jaws. Then it sprang high, over the heads of the gods, and it ran off into the cave-darkness and would not be seen in Asgard again, not until the end of everything.

The gods forced Loki on to the three great stones: they put one of the stones beneath his shoulders, one under his loins, and one beneath his knees. The gods took Narfi's spilled entrails, and they pushed them through the holes they had made in the stones, binding Loki's neck and shoulders tightly. They wound the entrails of his son around his loins and his hips, tied his knees and legs so tightly he could barely move. Then the gods transformed the intestines of Loki's murdered son into fetters so tight and so hard that they might have been iron.

Sigyn, Loki's wife, had watched as her husband was bound in the entrails of their son, and she said nothing. She wept silently to herself for the pain of her husband, for the death and the dishonour of their sons. She held a bowl, although she did not yet know why. Before the gods had brought her there, they had told her to go to her kitchen and bring the biggest bowl she had.

Skadi, giant daughter of dead Thiazi, wife of Njord of the beautiful feet, came into the cave then. She carried something huge in her hands, something that writhed and twisted. She bent over Loki and placed the thing she carried above him, winding it about the stalactites that hung from the ceiling of the cave, so that its head was just above Loki's own.

It was a snake, cold of eye, its tongue flickering, its fangs dripping with poison. It hissed, and a drop of poison from its mouth dripped on to Loki's face, making his eyes burn.

Loki screamed and contorted, writhing and twisting in pain. He tried to get out of the way, to move his head from beneath the poison. The bonds that had once been the entrails of his own son held him tightly.

One by one the gods left that place, with grimly satisfied looks on their faces. Soon only Kvasir was left. Sigyn looked at her bound husband and at the disemboweled corpse of her wolf-murdered son.

"What are you going to do to me?" she asked.

"Nothing," said Kvasir. "You are not being punished. You may do whatever you wish." And then even he left that place.

Another drop of the serpent's venom dripped on to Loki's face, and he screamed and threw himself about, writhing in his bonds. The earth itself shook at Loki's threshing.

Sigyn took her bowl and went to her husband. She said nothing—what was there to say?—but she stood beside Loki's head, with tears in her eyes, and caught each drop of poison as it fell from the snake's fangs into her bowl.

This all happened long, long ago, in time out of mind, in the days when the gods still walked the earth. So long ago that the mountains of those days have worn away and the deepest lakes have become dry land.

Sigyn still waits beside Loki's head as she did then, staring at his beautiful, twisted face.

The bowl she holds fills slowly, one drop at a time, but eventually the poison fills the bowl to the brim. It is then and only then that Sigyn turns away from Loki. She takes the bowl and pours the venom away, and while she is gone, the snake's poison falls on to Loki's face and into his eyes. He convulses then, jerks and judders, jolts and twists and writhes, so much that the whole earth shakes.

When that happens, we here in Midgard call it an earthquake.

They say that Loki will be bound there in the darkness beneath the earth, and Sigyn will be with him, holding the bowl to catch the poison above his face and whispering that she loves him, until Ragnarok comes and brings the end of days.

RAGNAROK: THE FINAL DESTINY OF THE GODS

I

U ntil now I have told you of things that have happened in the past—things that happened a long
time ago.

Now I shall tell you of the days to come.

I shall tell you how it will end, and then how it will begin
once more. These are dark days I will tell you of, dark days
and hidden things, concerning the ends of the earth and
the death of the gods. Listen, and you will learn.

This is how we will know that the end times are upon
us. It will be far from the age of the gods, in the time of
men. It will happen when the gods all sleep, every god
but all-seeing Heimdall. He will watch everything as it
begins, although he will be powerless to prevent what he
sees from happening.

It will begin with the winter.

This will not be a normal winter. The winter will begin,
and it will continue, winter following winter. There will
be no spring, no warmth. People will be hungry and they

will be cold and they will be angry. Great battles will take place, all across the world.

Brothers will fight brothers, fathers will kill sons. Mothers and daughters will be set against each other. Sisters will fall in battle with sisters, and will watch their children murder each other in their turn.

This will be the age of cruel winds, the age of people who become as wolves, who prey upon each other, who are no better than wild beasts. Twilight will come to the world, and the places where the humans live will fall into ruins, flaming briefly, then crashing down and crumbling into ash and devastation.

Then, when the few remaining people are living like animals, the sun in the sky will vanish, as if eaten by a wolf, and the moon will be taken from us too, and no one will be able to see the stars any longer. Darkness will fill the air, like ashes, like mist.

This will be the time of the terrible winter that will not end, the Fimbulwinter.

There will be snow driving in from all directions, fierce winds, and cold colder than you have ever imagined cold could be, an icy cold so cold your lungs will ache when you breathe, so cold that the tears in your eyes will freeze. There will be no spring to relieve it, no summer, no autumn. Only winter, followed by winter, followed by winter.

After that there will come the time of the great earthquakes. The mountains will shake and crumble. Trees will fall, and any remaining places where people live will be destroyed.

The earthquakes will be so great that all bonds and shackles and fetters will be destroyed.

All of them.

Fenrir, the great wolf, will free himself from his shackles. His mouth will gape: his upper jaw will reach the heavens, the lower jaw will touch the earth. There is nothing he cannot eat, nothing he will not destroy. Flames come from his eyes and his nostrils.

Where Fenris Wolf walks, flaming destruction follows.

There will be flooding too, as the seas rise and surge on to the land. Jormungundr, the Midgard serpent, huge and dangerous, will writhe in its fury, closer and closer to the land. The venom from its fangs will spill into the water, poisoning all the sea life. It will spatter its black poison into the air in a fine spray, killing all the seabirds that breathe it.

There will be no more life in the oceans, where the Midgard serpent writhes. The rotted corpses of fish and of whales, of seals and sea monsters, will wash in the waves.

All who see the brothers Fenrir the wolf and the Midgard serpent, the children of Loki, will know death.

That is the beginning of the end.

The misty sky will split apart, with the sound of children screaming, and the sons of Muspell will ride down from the heavens, led by Surtr, the fire giant, holding high his sword, which burns so brightly no mortal can look upon it. They will ride across the rainbow bridge, across Bifrost, and the rainbow will crumble as they ride, its once-bright colours becoming shades of charcoal and of ash.

There will never be another rainbow.

Cliffs will crumble into the sea.

Loki, who will have escaped from his bonds beneath the earth, will be the helmsman of the ship called *Naglfar*. This is the biggest ship there will ever have been: it is built of the fingernails of the dead. *Naglfar* floats upon the flooded seas. The crew looks out and sees only dead things, floating and rotting on the surface of the ocean.

Loki steers the ship, but its captain will be Hrym, leader of the frost giants. The surviving frost giants all follow Hrym, huge and inimical to humanity. They are Hrym's soldiers in the final battle.

Loki's troops are the legions of Hel. They are the uneasy dead, the ones who died shameful deaths, who will return to the earth to fight once more as walking corpses, determined to destroy anything that still loves and lives above the earth.

All of them, giants and the dead and the burning sons of Muspell, will travel to the battle plain called Vigrid. Vigrid is huge: three hundred miles across. Fenris Wolf pads his way there also, and the Midgard serpent will navigate the flooded seas until it too is close to Vigrid, then it will writhe up on to the sand and force itself ashore—only its head and the first mile or so of its body. Most of it will remain in the sea.

They will form themselves into battle order: Surtr and the sons of Muspell will be there in flames; the warriors of Hel and Loki will be there from beneath the earth; the frost giants will be there, Hrym's troops, the mud freezing where they stand. Fenrir will be with them, and the Midgard serpent. The worst enemies that the mind can imagine will be there that day.

Heimdall will have seen all this as it occurs. He sees everything, after all: he is the watchman of the gods. Now, and only now, he acts.

Heimdall will blow the Gjallerhorn, the horn that once was Mimir's, and he will blow it with all his strength. Asgard shakes with its noise, and it is then that the sleeping gods will wake, and they will reach for their weapons and assemble beneath Yggdrasil, at Urd's well, to receive the blessing and the counsel of the norns.

Odin will ride the horse Sleipnir to Mimir's well to ask the head of Mimir for counsel, for himself and for the gods. Mimir's head will whisper its knowledge of the future to Odin, just as I am telling it to you now.

What Mimir whispers to Odin will give the all-father hope, even when all looks dark.

The great ash tree Yggdrasil, the world-tree, will shake like a leaf in the wind, and the Aesir and with them the Einherjar, all the warriors who died good deaths in battle, will dress for war, and together they will ride out to Vigrid, the final battlefield.

Odin will ride at the head of their company. His

armour gleams, and he wears a golden helmet. Thor will ride beside him, Mjollnir in his hand.

They reach the field of battle, and the final battle will begin.

Odin makes straight for Fenrir, the wolf, now grown so huge as to be beyond imagining. The all-father grips Gungnir, his spear, in his fist.

Thor will see that Odin is heading for the great wolf, and Thor will smile, and whip his goats to greater speed, and he will head straight for the Midgard serpent, his hammer in his iron gauntlet.

Frey makes for Surtr, flaming and monstrous. Surtr's flaming sword is huge and it burns even when it misses. Frey fights hard and well, but he will be the first of the Aesir to fall: his sword and his armour are no match for Surtr's burning sword. Frey will die missing and regretting the loss of the sword he gave to Skirnir so long ago, for love of Gerd. That sword would have saved him.

The noise of battle will be furious; the Einherjar, Odin's noble warriors, are locked in pitched battle with the evil dead, Loki's troops.

The hellhound Garm will growl. He is smaller than Fenrir, but he is still the mightiest and most dangerous of all dogs. He has also escaped his shackles beneath the earth and has returned to rip the throats of the warriors on the earth.

Tyr will stop him, Tyr the one-handed, and they will fight, man and nightmare dog. Tyr fights bravely, but the battle will be the death of both of them. Garm dies with its teeth locked in Tyr's throat.

Thor will finally kill the Midgard serpent, as he has wanted to do for so long.

Thor smashes the great serpent's brains in with his hammer. He will leap back as the sea snake's head tumbles on to the battlefield.

Thor is a good nine feet away from it when its head crashes to the ground, but that is not far enough. Even as it dies, the serpent will empty its venom sacs over the thunder god, in a thick black spray.

Thor grunts in pain and then falls lifeless to the earth, poisoned by the creature he slew.

Odin will battle Fenrir bravely, but the wolf is more vast and more dangerous than anything could possibly be. It is bigger than the sun, bigger than the moon. Odin thrusts into its mouth with his spear, but one snap of Fenrir's jaws, and the spear is gone. Another bite and a crunch and a swallow and Odin, the all-father, greatest and wisest of all the gods, is gone as well, never to be seen again.

Odin's son Vidar, the silent god, the reliable god, will watch his father die. Vidar will stride forward, as Fenrir gloats over Odin's death, and thrust his foot into the wolf's lower jaw.

Vidar's two feet are different. One of them has a normal shoe on it. The other wears a shoe that has been constructed since the dawn of time. It is assembled from all the bits of leather that people cut from the toes and the heels when they make shoes for themselves, and throw away.

(If you want to help the Aesir in the final battle, you should throw away your leather scraps. All thrown-out scraps and trimmings from shoes will become part of Vidar's shoe.)

This shoe will hold the great wolf's lower jaw down, so it cannot move. Then with one hand Vidar will reach up and grasp the wolf's upper jaw and rip its mouth apart. In this way Fenrir will die, and so Vidar will avenge his father.

On the battlefield called Vigrid, the gods will fall in battle with the frost giants, and the frost giants will fall in battle with the gods. The undead troops from Hel will litter the ground in their final deaths, and the noble Einherjar will lie beside them on the frozen ground, all of them dead for the last time, beneath the lifeless misty sky, never to rise again, never to wake and fight.

Of Loki's legions, only Loki himself will still be standing, bloodied and wild-eyed, with a satisfied smile on his scarred lips.

Heimdall, the watcher on the bridge, the gatekeeper of the gods, will also not have fallen. He will stand on the battlefield, his sword, Hofud, wet and bloody in his hand.

They walk towards each other across Vigrid, treading on corpses, wading through blood and flames to reach each other.

"Ah," Loki will say. "The muddy-backed watchman of the gods. You woke the gods too late, Heimdall. Was it not delightful to watch them die, one by one?"

Loki will watch Heimdall's face, looking for weakness, looking for emotion, but Heimdall will remain impassive.

"Nothing to say, Heimdall of the nine mothers? When I was bound beneath the ground, with the serpent's poison dripping into my face, with poor Sigyn standing beside me trying to catch what venom she could in her bowl, bound in the darkness in the intestines of my son, all that kept me from madness was thinking of this moment, rehearsing it in my mind, imagining the days when my beautiful children and I would end the time of the gods and end the world."

Heimdall will still say nothing, but he will strike, and strike hard, his sword crashing against Loki's armour, and Loki will counter, and Loki will attack with fierceness and intelligence and glee.

As they fight, they will remember a time they battled long ago, when the world was simpler. They had fought in animal form, transformed into seals, competing to obtain the necklace of the Brisings: Loki had stolen it from Freya at Odin's request, and Heimdall had retrieved it.

Loki never forgets an insult.

They will fight, and slash and stab and hack at each other.

They will fight, and they will fall, Heimdall and Loki, fall beside each other, each mortally wounded.

"It is done," whispers Loki, dying on the battlefield. "I won."

But Heimdall will grin then, in death, grin through golden teeth flecked with spittle and with blood. "I can see further than you," Heimdall will tell Loki. "Odin's son Vidar killed your son Fenris Wolf, and Vidar survives, and so does Odin's son Vali, his brother. Thor is dead, but his children Magni and Modi still live. They took Mjollnir from their father's cold hand. They are strong enough and noble enough to wield it."

"None of this matters. The world is burning," says Loki. "The mortals are dead. Midgard is destroyed. I have won."

"I can see further than you can, Loki. I can see all the way to the world-tree," Heimdall will tell him with his last breath. "Surtr's fire cannot touch the world-tree, and two people have hidden themselves safely in the trunk of Yggdrasil. The woman is called Life, the man is called Life's Yearning. Their descendants will populate the earth. It is not the end. There is no end. It is simply the end of the old times, Loki, and the beginning of the new times. Rebirth always follows death. You have failed."

Loki would say something, something cutting and clever and hurtful, but his life will have gone, and all his brilliance, and all his cruelty, and he will say nothing, not ever again. He will lie still and cold beside Heimdall on the frozen battlefield.

Now Surtr, the burning giant, who was there before

the beginning of all things, looks out at the vast plain of death and raises his bright sword to the heavens. There will be a sound like a thousand forests turning to flame, and the air itself will begin to burn.

The world will be cremated in Surtr's flames. The flooding oceans steam. The last fires rage and flicker and then are extinguished. Black ash will fall from the sky like snow.

In the twilight, where Loki and Heimdall's bodies once lay beside each other, nothing can be seen but two heaps of grey ash on the blackened earth, the smoke mingling with the mist of the morning. Nothing will remain of the armies of the living and of the dead, of the dreams of the gods and the bravery of their warriors, nothing but ash.

Soon after, the swollen ocean will swallow the ashes as it washes across all the land, and everything living will be forgotten under the sunless sky.

That is how the worlds will end, in ash and flood, in darkness and in ice. That is the final destiny of the gods.

II

That is the end. But there is also what will come after the end.

From the grey waters of the ocean, the green earth will arise once more.

The sun will have been eaten, but the sun's daughter will shine in the place of her mother, and the new sun will shine even more brightly than the old, shine with young light and new.

The woman and the man, Life and Life's Yearning, will come out from inside the ash tree that holds the worlds together. They will feed upon the dew on the green earth, and they will make love, and from their love will spring mankind.

Asgard will be gone, but Idavoll will stand where Asgard once stood, splendid and continual.

Odin's sons Vidar and Vali will arrive in Idavoll. Next will come Thor's sons, Modi and Magni. They will bring Mjollnir between them, because now that Thor is gone it will take two of them to carry it. Balder and Hod will return from the underworld, and the six of them will sit in the light of the new sun and talk among themselves, remembering mysteries and discussing what could have been done differently and whether the outcome of the game was inevitable.

They will talk of Fenrir, the wolf that ate the world, and of the Midgard serpent, and they will remember Loki, who was of the gods yet not of them, who saved the gods and who would have destroyed them.

And then Balder will say, "Hey. Hey, what's that?"

"What?" asks Magni.

"There. Glittering in the long grass. Do you see it? And there. Look, it's another of them."

They go down on their knees then in the long grass, the gods like children.

Magni, Thor's son, is the first to find one of the things in the long grass, and once he finds it, he knows what it is. It is a golden chess piece, the kind the gods played with when the gods still lived. It is a tiny golden carving of Odin, the all-father, on his high throne: the king.

They find more of them. Here is Thor, holding his hammer. There is Heimdall, his horn at his lips. Frigg, Odin's wife, is the queen.

Balder holds up a little golden statue. "That one looks like you," Modi tells him.

"It is me," says Balder. "It is me long ago, before I died, when I was of the Aesir."

They will find other pieces in the grass, some beautiful, some less so. Here, half buried in the black soil, are Loki and his monstrous children. There is a frost giant. Here is Sutr, his face all aflame.

Soon they will find they have all the pieces they could ever need to make a full chess set. They arrange the pieces into a chess game: on the tabletop chessboard the gods of Asgard face their eternal enemies. The new-minted sunlight glints from the golden chessmen on this perfect afternoon.

Balder will smile, like the sun coming out, and reach down, and he will move his first piece.

And the game begins anew.

A

GLOSSARY

Aegir: greatest of the sea giants. Husband of Ran, father of nine daughters, who are the waves of the ocean.

Aesir: a race or tribe or branch of the gods. They live in Asgard.

Alfheim: one of the nine worlds, inhabited by the light elves.

Angrboda: a giantess, mother of Loki's three monstrous children.

Asgard: home of the Aesir. The realm of the gods.

Ask: the first man, made from an ash tree.

Audhumla: the first cow, whose tongue shaped the ancestor of the gods, and from whose teats ran rivers of milk.

Aurboda: a mountain giantess, mother of Gerd.

Balder: known as "the beautiful". Odin's second son, loved by all but Loki.

Barri, isle of: an island on which Frey and Gerd get married.

Baugi: a giant, the brother of Suttung.

Beli: a giant. Frey kills him with a stag's antler.

Bergelmir: Ymir's grandson. Bergelmir and his wife were the only giants to survive the flood.

Bestla: mother of Odin, Vili and Ve, and wife of Bor. Daughter of a giant called Bolthorn. Sister of Mimir.

Bifrost: the rainbow bridge that joins Asgard to Midgard.

Bodn: one of two mead vats made to hold the mead of poetry. The other is Son.

Bolverkr: one of the names Odin calls himself when in disguise.

Bor: a god. Buri's son, married to Bestla. Father of Odin, Vili and Ve.

Bragi: god of poetry.

Breidablik: Balder's home, a place of joy and music and knowledge.

Brisings, necklace of the: a shining necklace belonging to Freya.

Brokk: a dwarf capable of making great treasures. Brother of Eitri.

Buri: the ancestor of the gods, father to Bor, grandfather of Odin.

Draupnir: Odin's golden arm-ring which, every nine nights, produces eight arm-rings of equal beauty and value.

Egil: a farmer, the father of Thialfi and Roskva.

Einherjar: the noble dead who died bravely in battle, and who now feast and battle in Valhalla.

Eitri: a dwarf who forges great treasures, including Thor's hammer. Brother of Brokk.

Elli: an old nurse who is, in fact, old age.

Embla: the first woman, made from an elm tree.

Farbauti: Loki's father, a giant. "He who strikes dangerous blows."

Fenrir or **Fenris Wolf:** a wolf. Loki's son with Angrboda.

Fimbulwinter: the winter before Ragnarok, which does not end.

Fjalar: the brother of Galar and murderer of Kvasir.

Fjolnir: son of Frey and Gerd and first king of Sweden.

Franang's Falls: high waterfall where Loki hid himself in the guise of salmon.

Frey: a god of the Vanir, who lives with the Aesir. Freya's brother.

Freya: a goddess of the Vanir, who lives with the Aesir. Frey's sister.

Frigg: Odin's wife, the queen of the gods. Mother of Balder.

Fulla: a goddess, Frigg's handmaiden.

Galar: one of the dark elves. Brother of Fjalar and murderer of Kvasir.

Garm: a monstrous hound, who kills and is killed by Tyr at Ragnarok.

Gerd: a radiantly beautiful giantess, loved by Frey.

Gilling: a giant, killed by Fjalar and Galar, and father of Suttung and Baugi.

Ginnungagap: a yawning gap between Muspell (the fire world) and Niflheim (the mist world) at the beginning of creation.

Gjallerhorn: Heimdall's horn, kept by Mimir's well.

Gleipnir: magical chain forged by dwarfs and used by the gods to bind Fenrir.

Grimnir: "the hooded one." A name for Odin.

Grinder: Tanngnjóstr, or teeth-grinder. One of the two goats that pull Thor's chariot.

Gullinbursti: the golden boar made for Frey by the dwarfs.

Gungnir: Odin's spear. It never misses its mark, and oaths made on Gungnir are unbreakable.

Gunnlod: a giantess, the daughter of Suttung, set to guard the mead of poetry.

Gymir: an earth giant, Gerd's father.

Heidrun: a goat that gives mead instead of milk. She feeds the dead in Valhalla.

Heimdall: the watchman of the gods, far-seeing.

Hel: Loki's daughter with Angrboda. She rules Hel, the realm of the shameful dead, who did not die nobly in battle.

Hermod the Nimble: a son of Odin. He rides Sleipnir to beg Hel to release Balder.

Hlidskjalf: Odin's throne, from which he can see the nine worlds.

Hod: Balder's brother, a blind god.

Hoenir: an old god, who gave humans the gift of reason. One of the Aesir, sent to the Vanir to be their king.

Hrym: the leader of the frost giants at Ragnarok.

Hugi: a young giant, able to run faster than anything. In reality, thought itself.

Huginn: one of Odin's two ravens. Its name means "thought".

Hvergelmir: a spring in Niflheim, beneath Yggdrasil, which is the origin of many other rivers and streams.

Hymir: a king of the giants.

Hyrrokkin: a giantess, even stronger than Thor.

Idavoll: the "splendid plain", on which Asgard was built, and to which the surviving gods will return after Ragnarok.

Idunn: a goddess of the Aesir. She is the keeper of the apples of immortality, which give the gods eternal youth.

Ivaldi: one of the dark elves. The sons of Ivaldi crafted *Skiðblaðnir*, Frey's remarkable ship; Gungnir, Odin's spear; and new, beautiful golden hair for Sif, Thor's wife.

Jord: Thor's mother, a giantess, who was also a goddess of the earth.

Jormungundr: the Midgard serpent. One of Loki's children and Thor's nemesis.

Jotunheim: Jotun means giant, and Jotunheim is the realm of the giants.

Kvasir: a god formed from the mixture of the spittle of the Aesir and the Vanir, he became a god of wisdom. Kvasir was murdered by dwarfs, who made the mead of poetry from his blood. Later, he came back to life.

Laufey: the mother of Loki. Also called Nal, or needle, because she was so thin.

Lerad: a tree, probably part of Yggdrasil, which fed Heidrun, the goat that gives her mead to the warriors of Valhalla.

Lit: an unfortunate dwarf.

Loki: Odin's blood brother, the son of Farbauti and of Laufey. The shrewdest, most cunning of all the inhabitants of Asgard. He is a shapeshifter, and his lips are scarred. He has shoes that allow him to walk in the sky.

Magni: Thor's son, "the strong".

Megingjord: Thor's belt of might. Wearing it doubles his strength.

Midgard: "Middle yard". Our world. The realm of humans.

Midgard serpent: Jormungundr.

Mimir: Odin's uncle and keeper of the spring of wisdom in Jotunheim. A giant, perhaps also one of the Aesir. He was decapitated by the Vanir, and his head still gives wisdom and watches over the spring.

Mimir's well: a spring or well at the roots of the world-tree. Odin traded an eye to take a sip of its water, scooped up in Heimdall's Gjallerhorn.

Mjollnir: Thor's remarkable hammer and most prized possession, made for him by Eitri. (Brokk worked the bellows.)

Modgud: "Furious Battler". She was the guardian of the bridge that leads to the land of the dead.

Modi: Thor's son, "the brave".

Muninn: one of Odin's ravens. Its name means "memory".

Muspell: the fiery world that exists at the beginning of creation. One of the nine worlds.

Naglfar: a ship, built from the untrimmed finger- and toenails of the dead. The giants and the dead from Hel who will battle the gods and the Einherjar at Ragnarok will travel on this ship.

Nal: "Needle". Another name for Laufey, Loki's mother.

Narfi: Loki and Sigyn's son, Vali's brother.

Nidavellir, also called **Svartalfheim:** where the dwarfs (also known as dark elves) live beneath the mountains.

Nidhogg: a dragon who devours corpses and chews on the roots of Yggdrasil.

Niflheim: a cold, misty place, there at the start of everything.

Njord: a god of the Vanir, father of Frey and Freya.

Norns: the three sisters, Urd, Verdandi and Skuld, who tend the well of Urd, or fate, and water the roots of Yggdrasil, the world-tree. They, along with other norns, decide what will happen in your life.

Odin: the highest and oldest of the gods. He wears a cloak and a hat and only has one eye, having traded the other for wisdom. He has many other names including all-father, Grimnir and the gallows god.

Odrerir: a kettle for brewing the mead of poetry. "Ecstasy giver".

Ran: wife of Aegir the sea giant, goddess of those who drown at sea, mother of the nine waves.

Ratatosk: a squirrel who lives in the branches of Yggdrasil and takes messages from Nidhogg the corpse-devourer at the roots to an eagle who lives in the upper branches.

Rati: the auger or drill of the gods.

Roskva: sister of Thialfi, Thor's human servant.

Sif: Thor's wife. She had golden hair.

Sigyn: Loki's wife, mother of Vali and Narfi. After Loki's imprisonment, she stays with him beneath the ground, holding a bowl with which she protects Loki's face from the venom of the serpent.

Skadi: a giant, daughter of the giant Thiazi. She marries Njord.

Skiðblaðnir: a magical ship, made for Frey by the sons of Ivaldi. It folds up like a scarf.

Skirnir: a light elf, Frey's servant.

Skrymir: "Big Fellow". A particularly big giant, encountered by Loki, Thor and Thialfi on the way to Utgard.

Skuld: one of the norns. Her name means "that which is intended", and her domain is the future.

Sleipnir: Odin's horse. The fastest of horses, eight-legged, the offspring of Loki and Svadilfari.

Snarler: Tanngrisnir, which means tooth-barer or snarler. One of the two goats that pull Thor's chariot.

Son: a vat for mead.

Surtr: a huge fiery giant who wields a flaming sword. Surtr existed before the gods. Guardian of Muspell, the fire region.

Suttung: a giant, the son of Gilling. He takes vengeance on his parents' killers.

Svadilfari: a horse belonging to the master builder who built Asgard's wall. Father of Sleipnir.

Thiazi: a giant who disguises himself as an eagle to kidnap Idunn. Father to Skadi.

Thokk: old woman, whose name means "gratitude" but is the single living creature who won't mourn the death of Balder.

Thor: Odin's red-bearded son, Aesir god of thunder. The strongest of the gods.

Thrud: Thor's daughter, "the powerful".

Thrym: lord of the ogres, who wanted Freya for his bride.

Tyr: the one-handed god of war, a son of Odin; the stepson of Hymir the giant.

Ullr: Thor's stepson. A god who hunts with bow and arrow and who skis.

Urd: "Fate". One of the three norns. She determines our past.

Urd's well: the well in Asgard tended by the norns.

Utgard: the "outyard". A wild region of giants, with a castle at its centre, also called Utgard.

Utgardaloki: the king of the giants of Utgard.

Valhalla: Odin's hall, where the noble dead who die bravely in battle feast.

Vali: there are two gods named Vali. One is a son of Loki and Sigyn, who becomes a wolf and kills his brother, Narfi. The other is a son of Odin and Rind, conceived to avenge Balder's death.

Valkyries: "Choosers of the slain". Odin's handmaidens, who collect the souls of the dead who die bravely on the battlefield and bring them to Valhalla.

Vanaheim: the realm of the Vanir.

Var: goddess of marriage.

Ve: Odin's brother, a son of Bor and Bestla.

Verdandi: one of the norns. Her name means "becoming", and she determines our present.

Vidar: Odin's son. The silent and reliable god. One of his shoes is made from all the cast-off scrap leather of all the shoes that have been made.

Vigrid: the plain where the great battle of Ragnarok will take place.

Vili: Odin's brother, a son of Bor and Bestla.

Yggdrasil: the world-tree.

Ymir: the first being, a giant bigger than worlds, the ancestor of all giants. Ymir was nourished by the first cow, Audhumla.

NOTES

The *Poetic* (or *Elder*) *Edda* is a collection of anonymous poems in Old Norse, some mythological and some poetic. The most famous and most important of these poems is the Voluspa, sixty-six stanzas long. In it, a gigantic woman, a prophet and seer, imparts everything she sees to Odin.

Snorri's *Edda*, known as the *Prose*, or *Younger*, *Edda*, was written around 1200, and is in three sections: Skaldskaparmal, a book of instruction and explanation for skalds about the art of poetry and ways to use language in Norse poetry (which also contains a number of stories), the Hattatal, a catalogue of 102 different poetic metres, and the Gylfaginning ("the fooling of Gylfi"), in which Gylfi, a Swedish king, travels in disguise to Asgard and meets with its rulers, who call themselves High, Just as High, and Third, and asks questions, and receives many of the stories in this book as answers.

The *Prose Edda* was written by Snorri Sturluson (1179–1241). He was twice the Icelandic Law Speaker, the highest political office in the land. He lived as a politician and statesman, and was murdered at the age of sixty-two, by his son-in-law, for political reasons. He was also a poet and a historian. His most important works are the *Prose Edda* and the *Heimskringla*, a history of the Swedish kings that delves back into mythological times.

Edda is the Old Norse word for "great grandmother". So perhaps these are "grandmother's tales". There are other suggestions for the origins and meaning of *Edda*—that it comes from the Old Norse word for poetry, for example, or perhaps that that Edda means "The Book from Oddi". (The Oddi in this case would be the farm that Snorri Sturluson grew up on.)

Before the Beginning, and After

This is built up from the Gylfaginning in the *Prose Edda*, and also from the *Poetic Edda's* Voluspa, Grimnismal, and primarily the Vafthrudnismal.

Yggdrasil and the Nine Worlds

This is for the most part taken from the *Poetic Edda's* Voluspa and Grimnismal. That there were nine worlds is widely agreed. What those nine worlds were varies, depending on where you look.

Mimir's Head and Odin's Eye

This is a patchwork tale, built up from several different sources.

The tale of the spring of wisdom is found in the *Poetic Edda*, Voluspa, and in the *Prose Edda*, Gylfaginning. The wisdom of Mimir's head is from the *Poetic Edda*, Voluspa and Sigrddrifumal, while the story of Mimir and Hoenir is to be found in the *Heimskringla*, Snorri's collection of sagas about Old Norse kings, in the Ynglinga saga.

The Treasures of the Gods

These come from the *Prose Edda*, from the Skaldskaparmal.

The Master Builder

This is a retelling of a story from the *Prose Edda*, Gylfaginning.

The Children of Loki

From the *Prose Edda*, Gylfaginning.

Freya's Unusual Wedding

This is a retelling of a poem in the *Poetic Edda*, the Thrymskvitha, or the Lay of Thrym. It was the first of these stories that I wrote, and the first I ever read aloud to an audience. It was listening to the audience's reaction that gave me the impetus to keep going.

The Mead of Poets

This was an interesting story to retell. It feels like two or three different stories that have become attached, and the challenge was in trying to make them feel like one narrative. It's chiefly from Snorri's treatise on poetry in the *Prose Edda*, the Skaldskaparmal, and from the *Poetic Edda*, the Havamal.

Thor's Journey to the Land of the Giants

The question is asked, "Now has Thor never had an experience in which he encountered something so strong in might and powerful in magic that it was too much for him?" and in the *Prose Edda*'s Gylfaginning the question is answered.

The Apples of Immortality

Prose Edda, Gylfaginning.

The Story of Gerd and Frey

The most famous version of this story is from the *Poetic Edda*, a poem called the Skirnismal. In it Gerd objects to marrying Frey, and is threatened to make her change her mind. While I built the retelling from both versions, I chose Snorri's *Prose Edda*'s

Gylfaginning version for what happens when Skirnir tells Gerd that Frey loves her, in which she simply agrees to marry him. I prefer marriage without threats.

Their son Fjolnir is mentioned in Snorri's *Heimskringla*, Ynglinga saga.

Hymir and Thor's Fishing Expedition

I built this from two sources: the *Poetic Edda* poem Hymiskvida, "the Lay of Hymir", and the *Prose Edda*, Gylfaginning. Basically, the story is the poem, but the prose version has a longer and (to my mind) more interesting version of the fishing trip, and it's in the *Prose Edda* that Hymir cuts the fishing line.

Tyr is the son of Odin in the *Prose Edda*, but he is the son of Hymir in the *Poetic Edda*, so I compromised and made Hymir his stepfather.

The Death of Balder

Snorri is the main source, the Gylfaginning. There is more material in the poem Balder's Dreams, in the *Poetic Edda*.

The Last Days of Loki

One of the things I was really looking forward to when I wrote this book, was to tell the story of the Lokasenna, a poem from the *Poetic Edda*, "Loki's Flyting". And then, when I got there, somewhat ruefully, I covered the material I had been looking forward to making a chapter in a paragraph: it's what a drunkenly mischievous Loki says to the various gods and goddesses to upset them, and what they say back to him in their defence or to counter-attack. It's a wonderful poem, but it felt like it would have thrown the shape of the story off to have included it. This is built up from the Lokasenna and the *Prose Edda*, Gylfaginning.

Ragnarok: The Final Destiny of the Gods

I finished this book in a house in Hudson, New York, during the first blizzard of the season. The house had no Wi-Fi (and barely any furniture), and a power outage during the night made the first draft of the chapter vanish from my computer. I was sad, but wrote it for the second time, and it came out brighter; this time it found the ending in Snorri, at the end of the Gylfaginning. Snorri quotes extensively from the Voluspa in the *Poetic E∂∂a*.